Happily Ever After
. . . Almost

Happily Ever After

...Almost

A novel by JUDIE WOLKOFF

Bradbury Press
Scarsdale, New York

Family trees drawn by Herb Earle

Library of Congress Cataloging in Publication Data:
Wolkoff, Judie. Happily ever after . . . almost.
Summary: Eleven-year-old Kitty and her sister look forward to their mother's remarriage, but not to getting a stepbrother.
    [1. Remarriage—Fiction]   I. Title.
PZ7 .W8339Hap   [Fic]   81-18028
ISBN 0-87888-199-9   AACR2

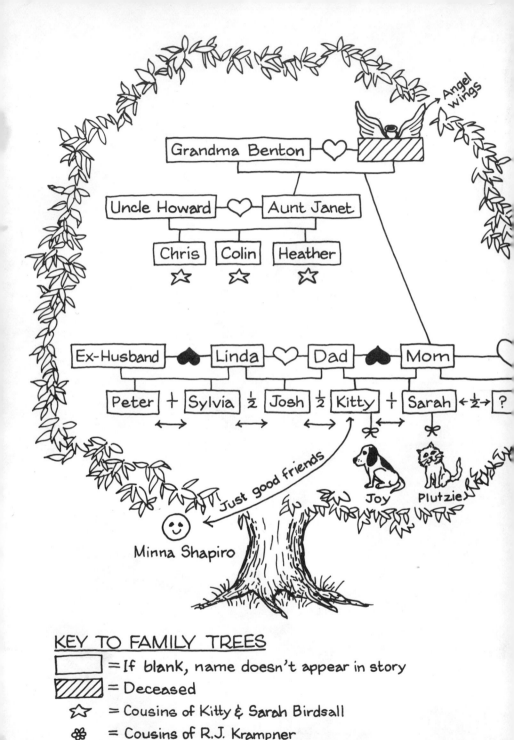

KEY TO FAMILY TREES

☐ = If blank, name doesn't appear in story

▨ = Deceased

☆ = Cousins of Kitty & Sarah Birdsall

✿ = Cousins of R.J. Krampner

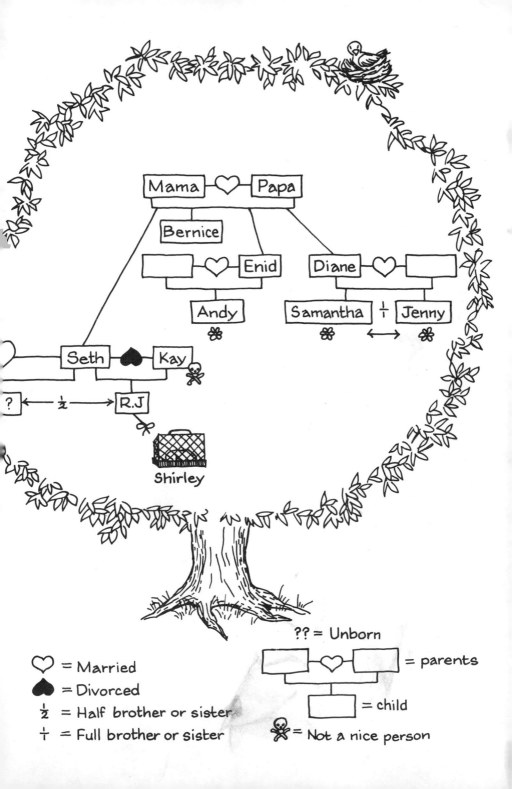

Mama ♡ Papa

Bernice

♡ Enid

Diane ♡

Andy
✿

Samantha ✝ Jenny
✿   ↔   ✿

Seth ♠ Kay ☠

? ↔ ½ → R.J

Shirley

?? = Unborn

□ ♡ □ = parents

♡ = Married

♠ = Divorced

½ = Half brother or sister

✝ = Full brother or sister

□ = child

☠ = Not a nice person

...1

Well, we made it! We survived our first year. We're alive and well—at least nobody's hospitalized at the moment. Our walls are up; the doors in. There's no more sawdust, no brrrat-a-zat drilling and we have a *real* kitchen. Gone forever are the days of washing dishes in the bathtub.

Better yet, Mom's marriage is intact. She and Seth celebrate their first anniversary next week. We won't be sharing it with carpenters. They hammered their last nail into place two weeks ago.

If I could, I'd climb to the highest rooftop and shout the news to the world . . . *"Hey down there . . . You hear me? Our renovations are over!"*

Eleven months of noise and rubble seemed longer than forever. Now we're in good shape. For a while, though, it was touch and go. Worse than the mess was the big rumpus over my stepbrother, R.J. He's had more problems than India.

Kay, his mother, is mostly to blame. Not too long ago, she and R.J. had a terrible fight. During the night he packed his bags, took Shirley his guinea pig and moved out of their big, plushy Upper East Side New York apartment.

Since then he's been living with us down here in Soho.

By us, I mean me, my quarter beagle Joy, Mom, my younger sister Sarah, her yellow tabby Plutzie, and Seth, our stepfather, who is R.J.'s real father.

By Soho, I mean the artsy-craftsy area below Greenwich Village in New York City where we have our loft: thirty-two hundred square feet on the fifth floor of an old shoe factory.

West, from my room, we overlook a warehouse with gargoyles. It's been converted into apartments and stores and I can spy on a hole-in-the-wall shop where a woman with frizzy pink hair makes tin vests out of soda can flip tops. Her name is Lottie. Next to Lottie is an African art gallery. Next to the art gallery is a health food store.

Sarah's luckier. Her room is on the northwest corner so she can see everything I can, plus a place down the block that sells glass eyes. "Eyes for All Occasions" the sign says. In the window, on Lucite cubes lit up with psychedelic lights, is a display of eyes ranging from some small enough to fit mice to one big enough for a giant squid. I've never figured out who buys them.

Every time R.J. walks around the neighborhood, he comes back saying that being in Soho is like being in a strange foreign country. That's true. It is. In fact, when we first moved here, I wrote my old friend Minna Shapiro that I felt like a tourist.

I'm not around much on weekends. Sarah and I like to take the train to Croton, a town in the suburbs an hour north of New York City. Croton is where our dad, a pediatrician, moved after he married Linda, his former nurse. We call our visits to Croton "playing musical kids" because usually when we arrive, Peter and Sylvia (Linda's kids) are getting picked up by their father (Linda's ex-husband) so they can spend the weekend with him and his new wife in Tarrytown.

The one kid not involved is eight-month-old Josh, who is bald. He's a half brother to Sarah and me on Dad's side. On Linda's side he's a half brother to Peter and Sylvia. Josh stays put on weekends.

When I think about it, Minna is probably my only friend who can keep our entire family straight. From the time I was three until last year, when Mom married Seth, Minna and I lived next door to each other on Hastings Street in Briarcliff, a town a few minutes south of Croton.

Minna knows who's who in our family, who lives where, who's related to who and how, which gets pretty complicated when R.J.'s aunts, uncles, cousins and grandparents are included.

They're not my blood relatives. Neither is R.J., of course. But our lives have been so scrambled together it seems as if we're related.

"R.J. isn't your average boy," Mom told Sarah and me when she first started dating Seth. "He's incredibly smart," she said, "so if you girls are patient with him, you'll find him fascinating."

That was a year and a half ago.

At the time we were still living in Briarcliff. Dad had already married Linda, and Mom was back at the job she'd had before Sarah and I were born—doing jacket layouts for Wesleyan Press, a publishing house that specializes in art books. Her second month there, she met Seth.

He's a photographer, of historical buildings mostly. The cover for his book on gothic cathedrals was one of Mom's first assignments. For her layout, she cropped the negatives of two of his black-and-white pictures, blew them up, then mounted them so they gave the illusion of gothic arches mirrored into endless space.

Sarah and I watched Mom work at home and the result was sensational. Wesleyan Press used her layout for the cover of their catalog as well as for Seth's book. When Seth saw the layout, he asked the art director to introduce him to Mom. Neither of them ever dated anyone else again.

Sarah and I had a sneaky feeling the first time Seth came to our house, carrying his camera and a muddy, yellow tabby kitten he'd found on the highway, he was going to be our stepfather someday. We weren't unhappy about it, either, which surprised a lot of kids.

I remember Minna once saying, "Aww, come on, Kitty . . . You don't have to cover for me. You must *hate* Seth! Nobody wants some guy who isn't their father living with them."

The truth is, you *do* want your own parents married to each other. But once you accept the fact that none of you will be happy if they are, you don't necessarily hate whoever else they marry.

From the start, Sarah and I thought Seth was terrific. Same with Linda, our stepmother. She's calm and organized, the kind of person who knows what she's cooking a week before she's hungry. Dad is a lot more relaxed with her than he ever was with Mom, who's been known to forget the laundry for a month if she's suddenly got a bug to frame weeds or something.

Mom's also moody. When she's up, she's game for anything. But when she's down (which Linda never is), she's as much fun as a black-eyed pea.

Dad always stopped talking to her when she got sulky, sometimes for days. Seth talks. And he makes Mom talk. Once when she locked herself in the bathroom, crying, he stuck a chair under the outside doorknob and hollered in to her, "Liz, if you don't care enough to let us know what's bothering you . . . you can stay locked in there!"

A little while later, a note scrawled in lipstick on a long stream of toilet paper slid out from under the door:

> Okay,
> I'll
> tell
> you!
> The
> renovations

are
driving
me
crazy!

(We were less than half finished at that point.)

and
Joy
chewed
up
Kitty's
new
retainer

and
while
I
was
showering
I
felt
a
lump
in
my
breast
and
I'm
scared!

Then a scrawlier P.S. written on a separate, shorter stream of paper slid out:

And
dammit
I
have
a
corn!

When Seth let Mom out of the bathroom, he wrapped his arms around her and she had a good, long cry, soaking the front of his shirt. "Honey, here," he said, handing her the phone. "Do something for all of us. Call a surgeon and make an appointment."

She did, and less than two weeks later, the lump was removed. It turned out to be benign, not the cancer we imagined. To celebrate, we picked her up at the hospital, drove straight to a midtown hotel and checked ourselves in. Then we had a four-day holiday free of pounding and hammering.

When we got home, Mom said her batteries were all recharged. She proved it by staying up most of the night, cementing tile in a shower.

A trait of Seth's I really like is his honesty. He's open and direct—even blunt sometimes—so when he's dealing with people who act phony, he calls them on it. Sarah and me, for instance.

When we first knew him, we were such goody-goodies it's a wonder he didn't get diabetes. Sarah laid the sweet stuff on practically to the point of curtsying. And I smiled so much my mouth used to feel numb. Normally, we're not that way at all. I'm an average to less than average smiler and Sarah's a royal pain.

I think what caused us to act unnatural was worrying about Mom. Since the divorce, she had been having more downs than ups. At times Sarah and I wondered if she'd forgotten how to laugh. With Seth suddenly in the picture, she was becoming human again. That's a nice quality to see in your mother. It means better lunches, with an occasional homemade chicken salad sandwich, fewer fights, going to bed feeling happy with a smile on your face and good talks when you need them.

Sarah and I were pretty anxious to keep Seth around.

One night after he drove up from the city where he lived and Sarah met him at the door with her usual, "Good evening, Mr. Krampner. May I get you a glass of ice water?" he took us aside and said, "Look, I'd really appreciate it if you girls were yourselves. I like real people . . . not angels, okay? And that includes real little people."

It wasn't said in a mean way, but it took us by surprise.

"And another thing," he continued, "your mother is a dynamite lady. You ought to have more faith in her . . . Know what I mean?"

We did.

"Maybe I will have that glass of water, after all," he said. "Speeches make me dry."

Sarah started for the kitchen, then stopped, looking over her shoulder at him. For a second I expected her to yell that he could darn well go get the water himself.

But she said, "Still want ice in it, Mr. Krampner?"

"Sure, if the ice is handy," he said. "And if we're going to get to know each other better, 'Mr. Krampner' is a bit formal, don't you think?"

"What would you like us to call you?" I asked.

"Seth'll do," he said.

"*Setheldoo?*" Sarah's voice went high, out of control, saying it. "Sure. Setheldoo's fine with me."

Sometimes even now when we fool around, we call him Setheldoo. The name has a special meaning for us because of what happened later that night.

Instead of going out to dinner by themselves, Seth and Mom canceled our baby sitter and stayed home to cook us meatballs and spaghetti. It was his idea, which made Sarah and me like him even better. Mom had had dates who couldn't wait to get away from us.

After dinner, Seth lit a fire in the fireplace and we toasted marshmallows. Then we had a good time together telling jokes and playing charades till long past bedtime.

Sarah and I weren't a bit tired when they took us upstairs to tuck us in. As soon as they went downstairs, we got out of bed and sat on the steps. The lights were out down in the living room; we couldn't see, but we could hear. It took a while, though, before their conversation got interesting. At first there was nothing but long pauses.

"Think they're kissing?" I whispered to Sarah.

9

"Uh-uh. Mom wouldn't do that."

I wasn't so sure. Both of us leaned closer to the banister, listening. After an especially long, quiet pause, we heard Seth ask Mom if she would ever like to live in the city.

"Yes, I'd love to . . . in a loft in Soho," she said. "One of my dreams is to renovate."

"What?" he asked. "A big, raw space in a converted factory?"

"From scratch," Mom said.

There was another long pause. Fifteen minutes, maybe. Sarah and I were getting so bored, we were ready to go back to bed. Luckily, Seth said something that stopped us. He told Mom he loved her. Then he asked her to marry him.

I remember Sarah kept whispering, "Say yes, Mom . . . Say yes."

Down on the couch in the living room, Seth was saying, "Liz, I know this is sudden . . ."

"No, it isn't," whispered Sarah, next to me. "We've been expecting it."

"You don't have to answer now," said Seth. "But I'd like you to think about it."

"We've thought about it," said Sarah.

Mom wasn't saying anything. She was so quiet, I wondered if she had fallen asleep. I wanted to go poke her, then finally she said, "Seth, I'd love to marry you . . . more than you can imagine. But don't you think we ought to get the kids together before we decide?"

Sarah groaned. "Why *now?* She's never been practical in her life!"

"Ssshhhh!" I was missing Seth's answer.

" . . . I know. I've been thinking how we should do it," he said. "Would you like me to bring R.J. up here some weekend? Or would you rather bring Kitty and Sarah to New York?"

"Bring Kitty and Sarah to New York," Sarah whispered.

"Maybe neutral territory would be better," said Mom.

Sarah nudged me. "Where's *that?*"

I was afraid if we sat on the steps any longer, we'd get caught. "C'mon," I said, tiptoeing upstairs.

Sarah scooped up Plutzie who had curled up on her lap, and came tiptoeing after me. "Just think," she said, following me into my room, "our very own wedding!" Then she whirled around and around in her nightgown. "Long dresses, bouquets . . . a honeymoon! You want to be a flower girl, or do you want to carry Mom's train?"

She did a half whirl, then stopped, watching me run my tongue over my braces. "Hmmm. Those don't look too good," she said. "Maybe Mom will let you wear a veil."

I got into bed. "Maybe Mom won't have a wedding. She's not deciding till we meet R.J. And we might not like him.

Sarah was up on her toes, dancing backwards. "Sure we will," she said, strewing pretend petals on my covers. "Mom says he's fascinating."

...2

We found out the truth the next weekend.

Seth called on Tuesday, to tell us he had tickets for the big Army-Air Force game at West Point, Saturday. "I thought it might be fun if we all went to root for the Air Force Falcons," he said. "They need our support . . . They're the underdogs."

Sarah and I knew better. We weren't going to root. It was to see how well we got along with R.J.

She and Mom and I drove to West Point from Briarcliff, a forty mile ride north along the Hudson River. Seth and R.J., meanwhile, were driving south from the Catskill Mountains. Rather than make the long trip from the city Saturday morning, they drove up Friday night and stayed in a hotel.

Our plan was to meet at the lake across from Mitchie Stadium.

I could tell Mom was tense. She's not a gum-chewer, but she was chewing gum anyway, and the closer we got to West Point, the faster she chewed. "Now remember," she said, "R.J. is sensitive . . . extremely sensitive. Sometimes it's easy to misunderstand him."

"So what do you want us to do?" I asked. "Be ourselves? Seth does. He said so last week."

Mom had to think. "Yes . . . yes, of course, be yourselves. But be nice."

"We can't please everybody," said Sarah.

"Try," Mom said as we drove past the guards at the gates.

Cars were lined up bumper to bumper in every direction. On big game days, West Point gets as jammed as Jones Beach in August. Even the crowds look the same—lots of kids running around; grown-ups with picnic baskets. Only they're all dressed warmer.

"This is a very famous military academy," Mom said as she turned a corner, looking for a parking space. "Robert E. Lee went here, so did General MacArthur, President Grant, Eisen . . ."

Sarah and I were more interested in finding Seth's little red sports car than in getting a history lesson. Somehow I knew in advance R.J. would be a pale kid with a vitamin deficiency.

Parking was trickier than sticking sixteen eggs in a twelve egg carton. Mom had to give up the idea of parking near the stadium. She drove down a steep hill and pulled into a lot next to the PX, the Post Exchange where Army people shop.

"Darn!" said Sarah as we got out of the car. "I've looked and I can't see Seth anywhere. Maybe R.J. got sick. Maybe he fainted."

Mom dropped her gum in a litter can. "Just because I said he was sensitive, Sarah, doesn't mean he's sickly. They're here. Seth would have called otherwise."

"R.J. could've gotten sick on the way, you know."

Mom ignored her and crossed the street, brushing crumbs of the bread stick I'd been eating off her yellow sweater. On the other side, she took a deep breath of fresh air and looked up at the clear, blue November sky. "We're going to have a wonderful, wonderful time," she said in a moment of optimism. "The sun's shining . . . It's not too nippy. A perfect day for football. Perfect!" Then she started up the hill, walking so briskly, Sarah and I had to run to keep up with her.

Half a block away from the lake, we spotted Seth leaning against a tree, waiting for us. "Hey, he's got on a yellow sweater, too," said Sarah.

I'd already noticed. And I was thinking I'd die if he and Mom had planned his 'n' her outfits. I was relieved when Mom laughed. That meant she was surprised.

"Hey, Setheldoo," Sarah yelled. She spurted ahead, nearly trampling a bunch of cadets in Army grays who had crossed the street. Mom and I cut around them and I saw her put her hand to her lips as she looked ahead.

"Oh, oh, Kitty . . . Seth's alone," she said. "R.J. isn't with him."

Once I got in front of the last cadet, I could see she wasn't kidding. Seth was hugging Sarah and nobody was with them. "See? What did I tell you?" Sarah hollered to us. "R.J. *did* get sick . . . *carsick!*"

Mom and I ran the rest of the way. Seth told us not to worry when we met up with him. "R.J. was a little green driving through the mountains," he said, "but he's fine now."

"Where is he?" I asked.

"Watching the warm-ups," he said between kisses for Mom and me. "We got here early."

We followed him into the stadium, up the sidelines toward our seats, which were left of midfield next to the Air Force Band, facing the sun.

Heading that way, I saw a kid sitting by himself, saving four seats. I knew it was R.J. Not only because he was saving the right number of seats, but because he was my age, eleven at the time. Mom had told me he was two months older. And I have to admit I was surprised. He looked normal. Not pale, thin, green or anything. Minna would classify him as "cute."

"There's R.J.," I said, pointing him out to Sarah.

She burst into a big grin. "Hey, R.J. . . . Hi! It's us," she shouted. Then she pushed her way up the aisle and stepped over a dozen people in his row to reach him.

I would have followed her, but I suddenly realized that Mom and Seth weren't behind me. They had continued on up the steps, through the crowds, and I could see Mom in her yellow sweater, waving at somebody up near the Air Force drummer.

Confused, I called to Sarah, telling her to come

back. She didn't hear me. She was talking a mile a minute to the cute kid saving four seats and he was shaking his head.

"Boy, Kitty . . . I'll never trust you again!" she spit out after she had elbowed her way back to the aisle.

I let her take the lead and followed her up to the row Mom and Seth had just squeezed into. "Look over there," she said, wheeling around to face me. "That's the *real* R.J.!"

There wasn't much to see. The only part of his body he had exposed was his pointy nose. The rest was completely bundled up, hidden inside a big, thick red plaid car blanket. A corner was lumped over his head and shoulders and the fringe hung limp above his eyes. I couldn't even tell if he had a neck.

"Well, go on . . . go in," I said to Sarah.

She stood fixed in the aisle blocking some kids with blue and white pom-poms, waiting to get around her. "Uh-uh," she said, narrowing her eyes at me. "*You* go!"

I pushed, but she wouldn't budge, and I could see she wasn't going to. Finally, I gave in and inched my way forward, careful not to bump anybody's coffee thermos the way she had in the other row. Seth was sitting closest to the aisle. "Thought we'd lost you for a minute," he said. Then he smiled, pulled his feet back so I could pass, then Sarah, and said he was staying on the end in case any of us wanted anything from the snack bar.

"I'll have a hot dog, fries, hot chocolate, cotton candy and an Almond Joy," said Sarah.

16

"Make that double," I said.

"Later," said Mom.

She had taken a seat next to R.J. and it bugged me that she was too concerned about him to care if we were hungry. "There's nothing worse than car-sickness," I heard her saying.

"Especially when you get acrophobia along with it," he mumbled, shivering, through his blanket. "I always do in the mountains."

The last two seats were next to the band. "You want to sit next to R.J. or the drummer?" I asked over my shoulder to Sarah.

"The drummer!"

I sat down, stretching my legs so she'd have to climb over them, then glanced at R.J., thinking he might say something. Nothing. Not hello, how are you, here's mud in your eye . . . nothing.

"R.J.," Seth prompted, "these are Liz's girls, Kitty and Sarah."

"Yes, I know," R.J. said, watching the field.

"Oh, yeah? *How* do you know?" said Sarah. "You never saw us before, did you?"

"Sarah, please," said Mom.

"Well-l?" Sarah said to R.J.

"Did you know who I was?" he asked.

"Yeah . . ."

His two hazel eyes fixed on her. "Well-l?"

Good-bye wedding, I thought. We could call it quits and go home. Sarah was never going to be a flower girl. She didn't like R.J., he didn't like her, and I decided not to have anything to do with either of them.

I folded my arms and shut my eyes. The sun was shining straight in my face. With a little concentration I could spend the afternoon pretending I was lying on a beach in Tahiti. I relaxed, tuned out, and along about then, all ninety-six members of the Air Force Band started rehearsing "The Star-Spangled Banner."

Nobody was playing together and the noise made me jump.

"Thanks!" said Sarah.

"For what?" I said.

"For *that!*" she said as the guy next to the drummer clashed his symbols.

I offered to trade seats with her. She considered a moment, looked at R.J., then reconsidered. "I'll stay where I am," she said.

Down in front of the band the conductor was making signals for everybody to play together. Rehearsal was over. It was time for the real thing. I rose to my feet, placing my hand on my heart. Gradually other people began standing, facing the flag in the field. I couldn't wait to see R.J. unravel his way out of his car blanket.

Neither could Sarah. "Come on, R.J. . . . . You've got to stand," she said. "It's our national anthem."

"You don't have to if you don't want to. Not if you're not feeling good," Mom told him.

"I'm still a little cold," he said, hunching up inside his blanket. "With the wind-chill factor, it's less than twenty."

Mom tucked the edges of the blanket under his

legs and told Sarah and me to turn around and sing.

Sarah started to, then she looked over at Seth. "I'll bet some nice hot chocolate from the snack bar would warm him up. And as long as you're going down there," she added very quickly, "I'll have that hot dog I wanted and a large order of fries."

"And get mine with mustard and sauerkraut," I said.

"And make that *three* hot chocolates," said Sarah.

By the time Seth came back from the snack bar, the game was underway, with the Army's Black Knights leading the Falcons by a score of 3–0. I hadn't understood any of it.

"What have I missed?" Seth said as he sat down, doling out our orders.

"Not much," said R.J., which would have been my answer.

Then I heard him take a sip of his hot chocolate and proceed to give Seth a total replay from the kickoff. He told him what guy on what team had intercepted at what yard line. How many yards had been gained and who gained them. What penalties had been called and so on and so on.

When he was finished, he started explaining a bunch of stuff about something called offensive strategy to Mom. It made me mad. I shook off a cold fry he'd dropped on my sneaker and ground it under my heel, watching him as I did it. He had some nerve monopolizing my mom! She's *my* mother, I thought. She's seen football games before . . . Who does he think he is?

And why is she smiling?

I felt this tremendous itch to swing my foot over and kick him. But I resisted. Instead I let my leg bounce up and down a little and tapped my fingers. Of course R.J. didn't notice.

Only Seth did. "It's not so boring at half time, Kitty," he called over to me. "Wait till you see the trained falcons take off . . ."

As he was describing how the falcons soared into the air, about ninety percent of the crowd went wild, hurling hats and programs. None of the excitement was happening near us in the lowly underdog section. Army was up to something. I looked down the field and saw a guy bigger than a warship bulldoze his way with a ball toward this fencelike thing at the end.

The ninety-percenters went crazier. Army's band struck up and their cheerleaders hopped up and down the sidelines like their pants were loaded with firecrackers.

In front of Sarah a man puffing a cigar swore as the 3 on the scoreboard changed to 9. Old warship had made it. To me it looked as if he'd left a dozen battered bodies strewn in his path.

"Nothing like glorified violence sans the glory," I said, quoting the remark Mom always made to the TV screen when Dad had been watching boxing matches.

R.J. looked directly at me for the first time. "Are you a pacifist?" he asked.

"Yes! Yes, I am!" I said. "I don't believe in violence! Rough stuff is a wicked sin . . . I don't even like playing Red Rover, Red Rover!"

He shrugged, then looked back at the game, making my itch to kick him even fiercer.

"You want to go for a walk?" I said to Sarah.

"Where?"

"I don't care. Anywhere. The ladies' room maybe. We could put on Chapstick."

As we got up to leave, Mom told us she didn't want us to buy a lot of junk. We told her we wouldn't and kept our promise. All we had was cotton candy and sodas from the Chili Wagon near the entrance.

Eventually we came across a ladies' room not far from the main gate. I restyled my hair completely while we were in there.

In dry weather it's limp and sort of moplike around my temples. I swooped it all up on top and tried a lot of experiments with different parts. Finally, I solved the problem of how to keep it out of my eyes: I let the back hang loose, then I divided the hair in front into three sections—one wide section above my forehead where my bangs were growing out, and two smaller ones over my ears.

Sarah and the woman at the sink next to her, washing her hands, were glued to the mirror we were all sharing, watching my progress.

"What're you going to do now?" asked Sarah.

"Make braids," I said.

I tied the wide, center top braid with a broken blue balloon I found on the floor. Then I used the string that had been attached to the balloon to tie a small side braid. Nothing else was on the floor for the other braid, so I got out my nail clippers and raised my arm—there was a snag of yarn hanging from my sweater.

"No, don't! Don't do that, dear . . . Don't snip. You'll make a hole," said the woman next to Sarah. "What do you need? Something for the rest of your hair?"

I nodded and she told me to wait until she finished drying her hands under the dryer. Then she rummaged through her pocketbook, producing a large paper clip which she bent around my last braid.

"Is this hair style a new fad?" she asked.

"No, I invented it," I said and thanked her when she left.

Sarah's hair was next. It's the texture of barbed wire and required four hands and two combs to redo it. While I removed her barrettes, she worked on her snarls, crabbing nonstop about some horrid puffy spot. "Look at it," she whined. "I comb and comb and the stupid thing won't flatten!"

"Then dampen it," I said. "If it's a little wet, maybe you can train it to go down."

She turned on the faucet and I took out the new grape-flavored Chapstick I'd bought the day before at the drugstore. By circling my lips over and over and over, I got them smooth, glossy and slightly purple.

"Think this is damp enough?" asked Sarah.

As I rubbed my lips together, tasting grape, I felt water splashing on my legs. Sarah was pulling her dripping wet head out of the sink. "I said a *little*, Sarah . . . a little!"

"Okay, okay. I heard you! Hand me a towel, would you?"

I told her there weren't any. "You'll have to use the hand dryer . . . and it takes forever."

"Not if I squeeze out some of the water with my underwear first," she said, squinting up at me through strings of wet, brown hair.

I warned her not to, but she ducked in the john anyway, while I stayed at the mirror applying more Chapstick. "Darn! Now *they're* sopping wet!" she grumbled a few minutes later. "Darn! And so are my jacket and corduroys!"

She wanted to trade some of her wet things for some of my dry things, but I refused and yelled at her to hurry up and start using the dryer. "Mom's going to be so worried she'll have the military police searching for us," I said. "And besides, I want to watch half time."

Sarah came hopping out of the john pulling her wet, twisted navy corduroys over her leg, then turned right around and hopped back in again when a group of women cadets filed into the ladies' room. Luckily, they hadn't come in to do any grooming. They soon left and Sarah stepped, cautiously, out of the john, fully dressed and ready to go under the dryer.

"Your hair won't be too noticeable if I make braids," I said, pressing the button to get the dryer blowing. "But don't expect me to take the time to do anything fancy."

She knelt on the floor under the dryer, looking at the braid standing upright over my forehead like a whisk broom. "I don't *want* anything fancy!"

We both combed, each taking a side, yanking and pulling, me pretending I was a Colonial girl, carding wet wool. Then I started the braids, pretending I was spinning.

Sarah was shivering. "Think R.J. would let me share his blanket?"

"I doubt it."

"The selfish jerk," she said. "If Mom marries Seth, will he have to come live with us?"

I watched a stream of water roll down from her skull following the contours of her neck knobs. The dryer wasn't much good for hair. "Only if his mother dies," I said. "She's got custody of him."

"Let's say prayers for his mother every night," Sarah said.

I fastened her barrettes on the ends of her braids and she pulled away from the dryer to see herself in the mirror.

"You ruined me!" she started screaming. "You did it on purpose, Kitty . . . You ruined me! Those aren't braids, they're all twisty! And I *still* have that stupid puff!"

To calm her down, I let her borrow my grape Chapstick. "But use it quick," I said. Then I exaggerated and told her I thought I heard the military police outside, searching for us. "So hurry!"

She was in a panic and nearly ran the sticky stuff all the way to her ears, she was putting it on so fast. "What'll they do?"

"Make us stand in the middle of the football field till Mom claims us."

"But she might not recognize us," she screamed, running for the door. "Why didn't you tell me?"

I found my Chapstick where she dropped it by the sink and ran outside after her. She was nowhere in sight.

I called, got no answer, tore around the corner through the gates, up the first steps, looped my way around the handrail of the next steps and finally spotted her zooming along the walk at the bottom of our section of the stadium.

I didn't try to catch up.

The way she was running reminded me of the way Minna and I swam fifty yards back to the beach the summer her brother shouted, "Shark attack!" at us.

Sarah looked as if some sort of supernatural force had taken over her body. I would have stayed where I was, enjoying her flight back to our seats if I hadn't known I was going to get it from Mom.

Mom didn't have nearly the sense of humor about our trip to the ladies' room that Seth had. He doubled over laughing when he saw my hairdo, which wasn't quite the effect I'd intended, but Mom—wow! Mom didn't think anything was funny. Particularly Sarah's wet head and clothes.

"I told her to dampen her puff," I said. "Not drown herself."

"I don't care, Kitty, you're older and supposed to be more responsible. I was so worried I was just about to . . . *and look at you!* What's that lavender grease on your mouth?"

I felt my top braid collapse. "Chapstick," I said, watching the broken blue balloon bob between my eyes.

Something in Mom's expression told me to sit down fast and shut up. Then I realized our seating arrangement had changed. Sarah was sitting between Mom and Seth, bundled up, shivering, inside R.J.'s blanket.

So where was R.J.?

I looked over on the other side of Seth. *Was it?* Was he that boy in the tan parka, staring at me like I was humiliating him?

Yes, I was afraid it was.

I sat down in Sarah's old seat next to Mom, turning my jacket collar upright to hide my lavender mouth. Couldn't people stop staring at my hair? I was feeling self-conscious.

Now Mom was doing it. "Well, it's certainly exotic," she said. Then she sighed and turned her attention to Sarah who was bawling about the crawly, wet underwear she'd put on backwards. Mom slipped her arm around her. Then Seth slipped his arm around her.

"What do you think?" he said to Mom over Sarah's head.

Think about what? I wondered. Whether we had killed their romance?

"I don't know," Mom said. "What do you think, Sarah?"

Why *her?* Didn't anybody care what *I* thought?

The Air Force Band started playing "Off We Go" and I never heard anybody's answer.

Half time was about to begin; the only worthwhile event of the day. I leaned forward, watching two Air Force cadets come out to the field with hooded falcons on their arms. They were going to take off the hoods and let those beautiful birds soar high, high, high into the air . . .

Mom was tapping me. "Come on, Kitty. We're leaving. We're going home."

...3

I rode with Seth.

His car heater wasn't working and ours was, which is why Sarah and R.J., who were cold, went with Mom. As far as I could determine, the romance was still on.

Seth and R.J. were coming to our house to stay overnight. And later, if R.J. didn't get carsick again, Seth was going to make us his special enchilada dinner. Afterward, we might take in a movie.

"What about tomorrow?" I asked.

"We'll vote on it in the morning," Mom had said before the five of us split up by the lake across from the stadium.

We could either go to Skateland or spend the day in the city, museum-hopping. Or if anyone preferred, visit Sunnyside, the house in Tarrytown where Washington Irving had lived.

We did none of the above.

Fifteen minutes from home, approaching the junction of Routes 9 and 134, a truck carrying a load of lumber cut into Mom's lane without signaling. She was forced off the road, where her car hit gravel, skidded, plowed into a ditch, bounced up as if it were light as a pie pan, then came down on four wheels.

It was as fast as a bee sting. The truck didn't stop, didn't even slow down, but sped on its way. Seth and I saw it all happen from behind.

Mom was prying her door open when we rushed to the ditch. She was a little woolly-headed, but her only obvious injury was a red, wedge-shaped bulge on her forehead. From a flying object hitting her, she said, rubbing it.

Sarah, who climbed out, crying, after her, had several bruises on her chin from the radio selector buttons.

Last to come out was R.J., white as a bleached hanky. His pointy nose was sort of pointy-swollen-crooked and bleeding. "It's probably broken," Seth said, examining it.

He set up Mom's emergency flares to flag a state trooper. Instead he lured a long-haired motorcyclist in a silver Windbreaker. The two of them pushed, rocked and shoved Mom's car until they somehow managed to get it out of the ditch.

The engine seemed to run all right—the knocking noise was always there, I told them. And the body only had slight damages; a cracked side window and a dent on a front fender a little bigger than a mailbox.

Mom was too shaky to drive. The five of us couldn't fit into Seth's sports car, so he left it locked by the side of the road and drove hers. We headed directly for Phelp's Memorial Hospital, with me navigating.

"I could find my way there underwater with a bag on my head in my sleep," I assured Seth. "It's my dad's hospital."

In the back seat, Mom was tending to R.J. and Sarah. Racing along by our side, acting as our escort, was the long-haired motorcyclist.

At the emergency entrance, Seth thanked him for his troubles. The motorcyclist waved goodbye and sped off, pra-ba-booming his Honda into the distance as we went through the automatic sliding doors and down a ramp to the admitting desk.

Sitting there, all business, was the tiny, pinch-faced woman who's been the receptionist since the dawn of Man. She slid her glasses up her nose, recognizing Mom immediately. "Hello, Mrs. Birdsall. Are you here to see Dr. Birdsall?" she asked. Then she stiffened, remembering they were divorced. "Is anyone with you injured?"

I thought it was pretty obvious. R.J. was standing in front of her snuffling blood into a wad of tissues.

"My son," said Seth. "He's been in a car accident with Mrs. Birdsall and her daughter."

The receptionist rang for a doctor over her intercom. A few minutes later Harry Lange, an old friend of Dad's, came walking double-time down the corridor. "Why, Liz," he said when he saw Mom. "What's happened?"

She told him and a whirlwind of tests began. Sarah, Mom and R.J.—all three of them—were checked out for concussions, internal bleeding, that sort of thing. All negative. Then R.J. was taken to get X-rays of his nose.

While he was gone, the rest of us sat in a nearby vestibule, waiting. I'd played about ten games of tic-tac-toe on the cover of a magazine with Seth, when Sarah, who had been dry-eyed for an hour, bolted out of her chair.

"Daddy!" she cried and burst into tears.

Mom, Seth, and I looked up. *"Bob?"* Mom said.

Dad walked into the vestibule, putting his stethoscope in his pocket. "Harry rang me up in pediatrics," he said, reaching for Sarah.

She was crying to beat the band now. "Why're you here on Saturday, Daddy?"

"I was checking on a baby with pneumonia," he said.

"That's what I'm going to have . . . I'm soaked to my bones," she sobbed.

Dad wiped her tears, calmly inspecting the bruises on her face. "Harry said you'd been in an accident. Where was it? Did the car . . ."

He was directing his questions to Mom, but of course, Sarah took over. She told him bits and pieces of what happened in the ladies' room, mixing it all up with how she slammed her chin on the radio, so none of it made sense.

"And now I've got these twisties in my hair," she said, "and R.J.'s probably got a busted nose and it's all stupid Kitty's fault!"

"That's not fair, Sarah," said Mom.

Defending myself didn't occur to me just then. I'd seen Dad eye Seth, trying to place him, and I was feeling torn between them. Should I be loyal to Dad, I wondered, and pretend I don't know Seth? Or vice versa?

"You're Seth?" Dad said, extending his hand.

Seth shook it. "Yes, Seth Krampner . . . and you're Bob, of course."

Over and done with. They had met and I didn't have to choose. Cagey Dad had known who Seth was before he asked—he's too precise to make mistakes. He'd really listened when Sarah and I told him who Mom was dating.

Sarah was watching them the way I was. "Seth might marry Mom," she said, testing Dad's reaction.

"The other way around is more accurate," said Seth.

Dad's expression was one of mild surprise, but Mom looked as if somebody had just poured an ice cold soda down her back. "Blessed are the young," she said, sighing. Then she shut her eyes and rubbed the red bulge on her forehead.

Dad saw it and leaned over, asking her if she'd banged her head on the steering wheel.

"A flying object hit her," I said.

Mom nodded and looked up. "The object was a box of crayons."

"Well, you can't blame me," I said. "Sarah's the one who left the crayons in the car."

32

I expected a loud denial, but Sarah was out in the corridor announcing, "Here comes R.J.! And he's holding a big ice pack on his nose."

Mom sprang from her chair, followed by Seth, then the rest of us. "What's the verdict?" she asked Harry. "Is it broken?"

Harry shook his head and gathered us near a light to show us the X-rays. R.J.'s nose was badly bruised, with broken vessels, he said, but he expected the swelling to go down in a few days.

Sarah couldn't mask her disappointment. "You mean it's not even bleeding?"

"It's coagulating," said R.J., breathing through his mouth behind the ice pack. "Dr. Lange packed my nostrils with gauze."

Seth helped him slip into his blood-speckled parka and Mom zippered the front. "Aw, you poor kid," she said, patting his arm. "This hasn't been your day, has it?"

"No, it hasn't," said R.J.

I knew what Seth was going to say by the way he looked at Mom: "Liz, I think I'd better take him back to the city now."

"But what about our dinner, Setheldoo?" Sarah asked, then shot over her shoulder to Dad, "Setheldoo's what he says he wants us to call him," then back to Seth, "You promised us you'd fix your special enchiladas."

"Not tonight, honey. I will some other time when R.J. feels better," Seth said.

Dad walked us to the ramp at the bottom of the

emergency doors before going back upstairs to the pediatrics ward.

"By tomorrow you'll be more comfortable," he promised R.J. Then he shook Seth's hand again, telling him he was sorry they hadn't met under better circumstances.

"And what about you, Liz?" he said to Mom. "Are you up to driving?"

Mom said she was fine other than having a splitting headache, so Dad bent down to kiss Sarah and me goodbye.

"Take care," he said to both of us. Then his eyes strayed up to the balloon bobbing on the end of my center braid. He didn't say what he was thinking and I was grateful.

We waved to him as the emergency doors slid open for us. Mom already had the car keys in her hand. She said she was driving Seth and R.J. back to their car on Route 9, then she and Sarah and I were going straight home.

"But I'm starving," whined Sarah. "Couldn't we all just stop off for a pizza first?"

"No, Sarah. Seth wants to take R.J. back to the city now. We'll eat at home."

Of course Mom never dreamed that Sarah was going to get her way—that we would stop off for pizza. But then, she never dreamed that once we got to Route 9, we'd find that Seth's car had been stolen.

...4

I really liked that little red sports car, but we never saw it again.

To get back to the city, Sunday, Seth rented a car in Briarcliff. He drove that a couple of weeks, then leased another car until spring. Finally he gave up all hope of recovering his sports car and bought a small, green compact station wagon, the car we're still using.

As for R.J.'s nose, it healed. Mom hovered over him, keeping the swelling down with ice packs, from Saturday night till Sunday afternoon, while he and Seth stayed at our house.

Even Dad was concerned; he called Sunday morning. When Sarah spoke to him, she told him about the stolen car, the hour we spent at the police station reporting it and the pizza we had afterward. The only news left for me to tell was how R.J.'s nose was doing.

"Maybe I'd better take another look at it," Dad said. Then he drove down from Croton to see R.J. before Seth took him back to the city.

The accident probably would have blown over and been forgotten like any other daily crisis if it hadn't been for the rotten call Mom got Monday morning.

The phone rang at seven A.M. Sarah and I were still in our nightgowns, baking cinnamon rolls for breakfast, and Mom looked asleep standing at the counter in her red robe, putting together our school lunches.

As Sarah reached for the phone, I glanced at the clock over the kitchen sink, thinking it couldn't be Minna calling. It was too early.

Mom dipped a knife into a jar of peanut butter and yawned as Sarah answered. "Who is it, honey?"

Sarah shrugged. "I don't know. Some woman who barked, 'Put your mother on!' "

Mom cradled the phone under her chin, saying hello. Then the knife fell out of her hand as she started spreading peanut butter on a slice of bread. She was wide awake.

"But I don't think you understand the circumstances," she said to the woman calling. "I wasn't being careless, or even *subconsciously* careless as you're suggesting . . . A truck forced me off the road and . . ."

Sarah and I frosted our cinnamon rolls and ate them, listening. Mom wasn't getting much of a chance to say anything. The woman on the other end kept cutting her off.

36

After a few minutes, she hung up, looking pretty close to tears. "Who was it?" I asked.

"Kay. Seth's ex-wife."

Before she could tell us what Kay had said, she had to sit down and pour herself a cup of coffee. Then she couldn't drink it. Her hands were too shaky.

"Kay didn't think I had any business driving R.J. in my car," she said, pushing aside the coffee. "She said if I really believed the accident *was* an accident, perhaps I should read Freud."

"What does that mean?" asked Sarah.

"That she isn't very nice, Sarah. And she doesn't think I am, either."

"You are most of the time," I said.

Mom smiled, then said thanks to Sarah, who had saved her the cinnamon roll with the most frosting. But I could see her heart wasn't in the smile or the thanks. The call had really upset her.

"Oh, lord," she said, resting her chin on her hand. "I wonder if I'm tough enough to deal with a woman like Kay."

I kind of wanted to stroke the sleeve of her robe and tell her to cheer up, but Sarah was already running her hand around the collar. "Sure you're tough, Mom," she said. "You're tougher than any mother we know. You could beat up R.J.'s mother with one hand. And Kitty and I'd help you."

Mom put her arm around Sarah. "That's not the kind of tough I meant, honey."

"I think you're all kinds of tough," said Sarah.

Joy, my dog, was outside the kitchen door,

scratching to come in. "You know what *I* think," I said as I unlocked the chain, "I think R.J. made up a pack of lies about the accident to make his mother mad at you."

"*Oh, Kitty . . . He wouldn't! R.J.'s not that way!*" Mom seemed almost as upset with me as she had been by the phone call. "Don't ever think that," she said. "R.J.'s got enough problems with his mother . . . I've never told you about them, but he does. He'd never try to create more."

I wasn't so sure. And I planned on asking him a few questions the next time I saw him.

That occasion came up rather unexpectedly two weeks later. Sarah and I had just spent Thanksgiving and the day after with Dad and Linda in Croton. We returned home Saturday, thinking we were going to stay home. But as we walked in the door, dropping our overnight bags in the hall, Mom drifted downstairs dressed to the hilt.

She had on her green silk dress and the jade earrings that Seth gave her when his book came out.

"Hey . . . Where're you going?" asked Sarah.

"Not me, honey . . . us," Mom said, blowing on her wet nail polish. "Both of you hurry upstairs . . . Your baths are running. We're going someplace special for dinner."

I knew it practically had to be as special as the White House when I got out of the tub and found a pressed skirt and sweater laid out on my bed. "Where, Mom? You forgot to tell us," I said, watching her dig through my drawers, searching for socks.

"Flushing, Queens . . . in the city," she said, tossing me a pair of knee highs. "Seth's parents want to meet you."

"Is R.J. coming?"

"Sure he is. We're meeting him at Seth's," she said, dashing for Sarah's room with a pair of my last year's tights.

Two hours later our car was parked in front of Seth's building on MacDougal Street in Greenwich Village. We spent a few minutes inside, looking at his third floor walk-up apartment. Then he, R.J., Mom, Sarah and I left, got in his new leased car and headed for Queens.

R.J. had been a yack-yack with Mom in the apartment. He described every detail of some bone skates and a bronze sword hilt he'd seen at the Metropolitan Museum's Viking exhibit. But sitting next to Sarah and me, riding to his grandparents', he could have had lockjaw.

I didn't say anything to him until we were on the Queensboro Bridge.

"How's school?" I asked.

"Mezzo-mezzo," he said, looking down at the East River.

What kind of showoff answer is that? I wondered. *Mezzo-mezzo!* Couldn't he give regular answers?—I hate school. It stinks. Recess is okay—things a normal kid would say?

I wasn't talking to him anymore. Ever. Except

later, to ask him why he lied to his mother about the car accident.

I folded my hands, letting them sink into the sag in the middle of my skirt. Sarah was sitting the same way, with her knees spread further. I changed positions. I couldn't stand how my old red tights looked on her—like loose, wrinkled red skin ready to be shed. They almost made me sick.

"What's the matter?" she said.

"Nothing," I snapped, looking at R.J. looking at the river.

Everything he was wearing was neat. Neat navy blazer. Neat white shirt. Neat tie. Neat pants. Couldn't he even dress normally? Did he have to be so preppy?

I felt a toe brush my sock. "Get your stupid foot off my leg," I said to Sarah.

"I wasn't touching your stupid leg," she yelled.

I don't know who jabbed an elbow first—her or me—but whichever one of us it was, started a fight that lasted clear to Flushing.

At first Mom asked us to stop.

When that didn't work, she asked me why I was so cranky.

When I didn't answer, she made up excuses for me—I was probably tired from Thanksgiving, she said.

Gradually her voice got louder and louder. She told Sarah to move over, me to keep quiet and both of us to keep our hands to ourselves. Or else.

Finally, she lost control completely and roared

into the back seat, *"Break it up right now or I'm having Seth stop the car this instant and neither of you will go anywhere for dinner! Do you hear?"*

"Too late," Seth said, pulling up in front of a huge brick apartment building.

He never got mad at us and Mom never got mad at R.J. I wondered why. It was kind of interesting.

"That 'mezzo-mezzo' answer bugged you, didn't it, Kitty?" Seth whispered as we were going into the building.

I nodded. "I like people to use words I understand."

"Why don't you talk to R.J. . . . . tell him how you feel," he said.

I wasn't sure if I wanted to. R.J. would find out he knew more than I did.

Walking to the elevator, I kept an eye on R.J. Something was making him nervous. When he wasn't biting his thumbnail, he was clearing his throat. Waiting for the elevator doors to open, I saw little beads of sweat pop up like blisters on his upper lip.

"Don't you like elevators, R.J.?" Sarah asked as we all stepped inside.

"Never mind," said Mom. "A lot of people don't. Me included," she added, which wasn't true.

Sarah watched R.J. swallow as Seth pressed the eighth-floor button. "Do you think the cables will snap and we'll get killed?" she said. "Or do you think we'll get trapped without any air?"

R.J. kept his eyes fixed on the changing floor numbers, without answering her.

"Mmmmm. Smell that," Seth said, sniffing. "Mama must be making kreplach."

I sniffed but I couldn't smell anything.

"What's kreplack?" said Sarah.

"Krep-*lock*," said Seth. "You say it like you have a bone in your throat. It's a Yiddish word for little square dumplings."

"Yiddish? *I* know some Yiddish," I said for R.J.'s benefit. "Meshugga means crazy. My friend Minna's Jewish . . . I learned it from her."

The elevator doors opened. R.J. was the first one out and we followed the delicious smells down the hall to 8-B. Seth buzzed and a second later we were inside a small foyer being smothered by a gray-haired woman who felt like a dozen squooshy pillows . . .

"What's with your smashed nose, R.J.? It looks fine. You should see your grandma more often. And you, Liz? You're working hard? And these are your girls I keep hearing about? Such nice girls!" she said during one, long enormous hug. "Bring them in, Seth . . . Bring them in! I want Papa to look at them. Papa," she shouted, "*Papa . . .?*"

I didn't know what to make of her.

"You have to shout a little . . . Papa's a little hard of hearing," she said, clamping my hand in hers. "You're Kitty, right?" I nodded. "And you, darling, you're Sarah?" Sarah nodded. "Come!" she said.

Papa, Seth's father, was more reserved.

"We're here, Pop," Seth said when we found him in the living room.

"Oh, you're here," his father said like he'd just

seen us yesterday. "Sit," he told us, continuing to set napkins on the coffee table. Then he looked up. "You had a nice drive?"

"A little *meshugga*," I shouted before R.J. could beat me to something fancier.

Seth's mother spread cheese on a cracker and stuck it in my hand. "We've got another smart little faygeleh," she said, giving me an affectionate pat on the bottom. "Sit, darling. You sit on one side of me here on the couch, and Sarah, you keep me company on the other. Such nice girls," she said as we sat. "Tell me, do you get good grades in school like our R.J.?"

We both nodded, hoping Mom wouldn't contradict us.

"Of course you do," she went on, sticking another cracker with cheese in Sarah's hand. "Papa! The girls want something cold to drink . . . What do you want, girls? Soda? Lemonade? Juice? . . . Any kind you want. You want apple?" She took a breath. "I knew when you came in, you were smart girls."

"Lemonade!" I shouted for Papa.

"Soda!" shouted Sarah. "Cherry if you've got it!"

Papa readjusted his hearing aid. "Nice strong voices," he said, disappearing into the kitchen.

Sarah and I warmed up to both of them long before dinner. We could do no wrong in their house. Nothing. We were treated as special as R.J. Seth's mother—"Mama," Papa called her—had a philosophy that children, *all* children, needed praise. She even said so.

She was the first person outside my family, excluding Sarah, who ever used the word "beautiful" in connection with my appearance.

"Such a beautiful neck Kitty has," she said, setting kreplach soup on the table in the cramped alcove where we were eating. "Long like a swan. Greta Garbo should be so lucky."

I held my head high for the rest of dinner. And I ate everything she served. So did Sarah. She had two helpings of latke, potato pancakes, and kept her pinky up when she lifted her fork because Mama told her she had delicate fingers. Papa agreed. "Like a Balinese dancer," he said.

"Think I could ever be one?" Sarah said, crooking her fingers to brush her hair off her cheeks.

"No! You're not Balinese," said R.J.

"So what does it matter?" said Papa. "She'll study harder. Or if she wants, she'll be a surgeon."

Sarah liked the surgeon idea. I could tell by the way she cut up her chicken.

Neither of us could soak up enough compliments. We were gorgeous, delightful and clever and we did everything possible to encourage them to tell us more good things about ourselves.

I chewed with my mouth shut and admired Mama's blue picture plates hanging over the buffet. They were from Fredericksburg, Williamsburg, St. Augustine and Jamestown, she told me.

"Oh, I studied Jamestown last year," I said and acted out Pocahontas saving Captain Smith. "Please, Father . . . Please! Don't cut off his head! Take my life, Father, but spare Captain James Smith . . ."

"*John* Smith," said R.J.

". . . Please, Father. I beg of you with all my heart. Kill me! But don't kill . . ."

Mom said, *"That's enough, Kitty!"* But Mama and Papa and Seth laughed and laughed till tears came and Papa told me I was a born actress. Joan Crawford had never been so talented, he said.

Sarah's table manners were nearly as flawless as mine. She used her napkin, didn't suck the ice in her ice water and made a big point of seeing that Papa got his share of attention.

"What would happen if we all hummed?" she asked. "Would your hearing aid crackle?"

He said it would and she said sternly, "Nobody hum!" Then she asked him how he kept it in his ear. He showed her by hooking it around her ear. "You're so lucky," she said. "I always wanted one. My whole life I wanted a hearing aid."

Papa let her wear it while we ate dessert.

Sarah swelled with goodness at his generosity. She couldn't stop making compliments. Everything was nice. Papa's watch ticking. R.J.'s swallowing. The steam hissing in the radiator.

"I'll bet you were so nice you never spanked Seth," she said to Mama when she brought out coffee.

"Not because I was *nice,* darling. Because he was a good boy. Only twice he gave me reason to forgive him."

"What did he do?"

"He bit his baby sister Bernice's nose, the one

time. The other, he toasted toast. Three whole loaves of bread he toasted, trying out the new toaster."

Mama set the coffee tray on the table, then gave Seth such a hug with her round pillow arms, he almost disappeared for a moment. "Money for bread was scarce then," she said. "But how was a little pitzeleh two years old to know? Seth, darling, all my life I've been sorry I forgave you so hard."

Seth was laughing. "Now, Mama . . . You forgave me hundreds of times. You've forgotten."

"I forget nothing," she said. "From that day on, it was God alone I let forgive you."

This was quite a revelation for Sarah and me. We had never thought of punishment as forgiveness. When we got punished, we were punished period. No TV. No allowances. Extra garbage duty. And nobody ever forgave anybody.

The advantages of turning the burden of punishment over to God were staggering.

We begged to hear more stories of Seth's childhood, so Papa took a worn family album out of a cabinet and removed a picture.

"If you'll look on the left, you'll see the famous Mayor La Guardia," he said, pointing to a short, chunky man. "And shaking the mayor's hand," he said, sliding his finger to a young boy who resembled R.J., "is the little third-grader who won a citywide essay contest—'Why I Love New York.' You know what the mayor gave him as a prize?"

"What?" Sarah and I said together.

"A twenty-five-dollar bond."

Seth smiled with embarrassment as Papa handed Mom the picture. But Mom positively glowed. "Oh, honey . . . Look at you! Look at your proud smile," she said, letting on how much she loved him. "What did you write about? Can you remember?"

"And don't be modest," said Mama. "It was a beautiful essay."

Seth closed his eyes, thinking. "Let's see. I know I wrote about a street vendor who sold Chinese apples. And Pop's candy store . . ."

"You had a candy store?" I said to Papa.

He nodded. "With penny candy and twelve flavors of ice cream."

"And I listed every flavor in my essay," said Seth.

"Why don't you tell about your picture of the old men playing chess in the park?" said R.J.

"How'd you know about it?" asked Seth.

"Grandpa showed me," said R.J. "He showed me all your Brownie camera pictures the summer he taught me chess."

Sarah and I had to see the pictures. All the pictures. Not just Seth's old Brownie camera pictures, but every picture of every Krampner in Mama and Papa's possession.

We toured the apartment, seeing what was framed. Then we had Papa in and out of cabinets, up and down bookcases, collecting what wasn't framed—two shoe boxes of loose pictures and a stack of albums. When the last dish was cleared, we spread them on the table and sorted through them.

Mama and Papa's wedding pictures came first.

Then baby pictures. Then pictures taken at the summer cabin on Spoon Lake; Seth changing from a scrawny kid feeding a chipmunk to a muscular teenager, paddling a canoe.

Next came graduation pictures and more wedding pictures. Seth's oldest sister Enid's wedding was in one album. His sister Diane's was in another. There was a third wedding album, but I saw Mama put it out of reach on the buffet.

I eyed it, knowing it had pictures of Seth marrying Kay. Mama saw me. "Tell me, Kitty," she said, drawing my attention to a white album inscribed *Grandchildren,* "what do you think of our little rabbi?"

I looked at the picture of a baby sucking its thumb. "Rabbi?" I said.

"You mean you never heard the rabbi story? How R.J. got his name?"

R.J.'s head shot up from the pictures he was poring over with Papa at the other end of the table. "Don't! Don't tell her!" he shrieked. Then he dived for the album. "And don't show any pictures in here!"

His outburst floored Mama. For a split second she seemed stunned, then I saw a funny, knowing look register across her face.

"R.J. . . . . quick! Into the kitchen! My throat's on fire," she said, going into a sudden coughing seizure. "Oh, and such a fire," she added, banging on her chest. "Bring me a glass of water, would you, darling?"

R.J. pushed back his chair and Mama waved him down again. "No, better my cough syrup first. Behind the Epsom salts in the medicine cabinet. Get that . . . *then* the water."

As soon as he was out of the room, Mama leaned forward, tapping her head. "I'm seventy-three years old and still a dummkopf," she whispered. "The boy's upset. He's been upset since his mother called you, Liz. I wondered why he was touchy tonight."

Mom looked puzzled. "He knows Kay called about the car accident?"

"Oh, yes . . . He overheard every word," Mama said. "And cry! He called me from a pay phone on his way to school that day. You never heard such heartbr . . ."

"Which cough syrup do you want?" R.J. called to her from the bathroom. "You've got five different brands."

"Read the labels and bring one that won't put cotton in my head," she called back, trying to keep him in there longer. Then she looked at all of us again. "Such heartbreak from a young boy you never heard."

"Why was he crying?" asked Sarah.

"Because he was worried that you girls and your mother might think he'd exaggerated about his nose and the accident," said Seth. "He called me, too."

Now I was puzzled. "What's that got to do with his baby pictures?"

"Everywhere his mother's in the album," Mama whispered. "One thing leads to another. He thought if you saw her pictures, you'd talk about her. I wasn't thinking when I showed you and . . ."

"Ice?" R.J. called from the kitchen.

Mama coughed. "No, darling. Just plain water."

Driving home across the bridge, I felt guilty. Mom was right, I thought. R.J. was supersensitive. I'd misjudged him.

Except for a few hang-ups like using big words and being scared of elevators and being too neat and preppy, maybe he wasn't so bad. Maybe I could get used to him.

...5

I was wrong. And Minna told me I was wrong on our way to school one day the next week.

"Anybody who's chicken riding an elevator is a wimp," she said. "You'll never get used to him."

"You're scared of flying in planes," I said.

"So? That's different, Kitty. And the next time R.J. shows off with a fancy word . . . fix him! Say something fancier."

I told her I'd already used meshugga. "Do you know anything better?" I asked.

"No. But I'll look through the dictionary this morning."

When we met at lunch, she handed me a paper with *opisthotonos* and *floccinaucinihilipolification* written on it. She told me one word was a disease and she'd forgotten what the other was . . . but it wouldn't matter. R.J. wouldn't know it. Nobody would.

"So learn them."

"But R.J. might be nice the next time I see him," I said. "I might not have to use them."

"You will," she predicted.

Minna wasn't around at Christmas when Mom and Seth announced that they were getting married in May. But their engagement wouldn't have surprised her. I'd been keeping her posted on their romance. She knew about the proposal and she knew Seth. Every time he visited, she made a point of trying to be at our house.

Nobody else was surprised about the wedding, either. Not Dad, and not even Mom's mom, my Grandma Benton, who lives three thousand miles away in Oregon. On the phone she said she'd been reading between the lines in Mom's letters for months.

Sarah and I saw R.J. again during Christmas vacation. It was the first time we had gotten together since dinner at Mama and Papa's. Seth and Mom took the three of us skating at Rockefeller Center, an outdoor rink in the heart of New York City. Driving in with Mom and Sarah, I was anxious to try out the two long, flowered neck scarves I'd brought. I was going to tie them around my wrists and let them float while I skated.

I was sorry the scarves weren't silk. I was sure that's what Peggy Fleming had used on her wrists when I saw her in the Ice Follies. They had looked so beautiful. Like soft, pastel fantasy smoke quivering around her body when she did double axels.

My problem was, I couldn't do double axels. I kept trying at the rink. I flapped my arms, did the crawl stroke, the breast stroke and whirled my hands above my head, doing my best to turn the scarves into fantasy smoke. But my body wouldn't move like Peggy Fleming's.

R.J. was watching me. I knew he was. I'd seen him inch his way, stiff-legged, around the edge of the rink, watching. He couldn't even glide. I could, and I went gliding past him, smiling, as I tried an arabesque with my scarves fluttering.

"You've got a terrible need to be the center of attention, don't you?" he said.

I stopped, looking around to see who he was talking to. Nobody else was near us. *"Me?"* I said.

"Yes, you," he snapped. "You're a classic exhibitionist. You're not happy if you're not in the limelight every second."

I couldn't believe it. "Who . . . *me?"* I asked again.

"Who else, Pocahontas? I'm amazed you're not wearing balloons today."

I couldn't remember ever being more crushed. But I didn't want him to know. I yelled that he was a wimp and a chicken and a big boob and a preppy goon. "And not only that," I screamed, "I hope you come down with *opisthppss . . . floxxynoxxy . . .*"

The tears were coming. I was so mad at myself for not learning the words Minna gave me, I skated off. But not very far. I wasn't watching where my scarves were. They got all tangled in my skate blades and I took a spill on the ice, nearly killing myself. Well, not really. But one of my blades cut my shin. It was bleeding and we had to leave the rink.

Seth offered to take all of us to his apartment so he and Mom could bandage my shin. I refused. I wanted to go home.

When we got there, Mom washed my cut, rubbed antiseptic cream on it, applied a big Band-Aid and told me she was glad I hadn't needed stitches. I wasn't. I wanted a grisly scar to blame on R.J.

"He's the meanest boy I ever met," I cried. "I hate him!"

"No, honey, he's not mean," Mom said. "He's just trying to understand what makes you tick . . . It's perplexing him. You two are very, very different."

"Do you always have to take *his* side?" I said.

"I'm not taking anybody's side, Kitty. You and R.J. are the same age. There's bound to be some resentment beween you. His is naturally stronger . . . His father's going to be living with you and Sarah. He feels threatened."

"*My* father lives with Peter and Sylvia," I said, "and I don't feel threatened."

"But you did in the beginning, honey. So did Sarah."

I lay in bed a long time that night trying to remember how I felt when Dad and Linda got married. I'd always liked Linda. But now and then I'd had a pang that maybe she wouldn't be as nice to Sarah and me once she was our stepmother.

My memory of their wedding was blurry. It was a short, simple ceremony in a judge's chamber witnessed by a few friends and members of the family. That had disappointed me a little. I'd hoped it would be held in a huge church with organ music, lots of bells ringing and people throwing rice. But I hadn't been unhappy. By then I'd completely gotten over my old wish that Mom and Dad would fall in love all over and get back together again.

Linda was just as nice after the ceremony as she had been before. If anything made me feel threatened, it was little Sylvia at the reception. She was too cute.

Everybody in our wedding party had gone to a no-kidding-around posh restaurant in an old coach house overlooking the Hudson River. It was one of those dark, romantic places with candlelight, flowers and waiters wearing dish towels on their arms. Not many kids eat there, so they didn't have highchairs. Sylvia still needed one.

She wasn't even in nursery school then, but Peter, who was, suggested that she wait outside in the car while the rest of us ate.

Dad said no. So did our waiter, an old string bean of a man whose face looked like it had worn out three other bodies. He didn't smile once at Peter and Sarah and me. We could have sat on tacks and broken glass for all he cared. But Sylvia? He went totally gaga over her.

After he'd hustled up a couple of pillows to raise her to the table, he called her a little princess, then laughed like anything when she ordered, "Chitchen noodow thoup."

Dad had laughed, too, and it made me very uncomfortable.

The next couple of weeks I called him almost every day at his office, saying, "This is Kitty Birdsall. Remember me?"

He always did and I was always relieved.

Lying in bed with the cut from my skate blade stinging, I wondered what *exactly* was bugging R.J. enough to make him feel threatened. It certainly wasn't because he thought I was too cute. He'd made that clear. And it wasn't because he was worried Seth would forget him.

When Seth drove up to Briarcliff by himself a few days later, I asked what he thought.

"Why don't we go for a long walk and talk about it," he said.

Joy came with us and we took a path through the woods behind our house to a frozen duck pond a quarter of a mile away. The heavy snowfall we'd had during the night had eased up in the morning. It was coming down again, only lighter, and it was the kind of snowfall I liked—there was no wind.

The woods were so pretty and so quiet, I suddenly didn't feel like talking about R.J. Seth seemed to sense it and didn't press. He'd brought his Nikon with a special outdoor filter; I'd brought the pocket camera he'd given me as a Hanukkah-Christmas present. It was a good thing both of us were wearing boots. Under the new powder, the snow was deep and crusty. We sank in above our ankles.

Joy strayed off the path, sniffing out a hidden rabbit burrow, and Seth and I waited for her, making a game of who could come up with the most far-out description of snowflakes.

"Fairy clouds with spangles," I said.

"Sanitized dust balls," he said.

"Ant parachutes with holes," I said.

He took a picture of me shaking snow off a pine limb and I took one of him touching a funnel of ice poking out of a hollow tree stump. Then we followed Joy, who was leaping ahead of us to the pond.

No matter what time of year it was, or how I felt, I liked going to the duck pond. I'd gone there almost every day the summer Mom and Dad separated. But I didn't tell Seth, thinking it might make him sad. Instead I told him how Minna and I used to pack baloney sandwiches and take as many dolls as we could carry, then sneak through the woods pretending we were escaping evil people who wanted to lock us in a dungeon.

"But that was when we were little," I said. "Now Minna and I sit on opposite sides of the pond, talking to each other with her walkie-talkies."

"By the way, where is Minna? I haven't seen her lately," he said.

"In Florida, spending Christmas vacation with her grandmother. The Shapiros drove down . . . Minna's scared of airplanes."

His camera clicked as I caught a snowflake on my tongue. "I guess you've got some news for her when she gets back."

"You mean the wedding? No, I told her the day after you proposed to Mom," I said.

He laughed and hit me with a soft snowball. I packed one to throw at him, but Joy was dancing around me, yapping to play. I tossed the snowball out across the pond and she dashed after it with her little tail going so fast her whole rear end wiggled.

Seth got his camera ready to snap a picture of her.

"I bet R.J. wishes you and Mom weren't getting married," I said.

He looked at me, forgetting his picture. "No, not at all. R.J. was very happy when I told him . . . He's crazy about your mother."

"Well, I know he hates me!"

"Why? Because of what he said at the rink about your Peggy Fleming scarves . . . showing off and all?"

I nodded.

"Kitty, you might not believe this, but R.J. would love to be friends with you. He's a little intimidated. Scared. He doesn't know how to approach you."

I checked his face to see if he was kidding. He wasn't and I told him he was right—that I didn't believe him. "If R.J. wants to be friends, he sure has a funny way of showing it," I said.

We started back through the woods, walking slower than we had coming. Seth put his arm around me and told me some things about R.J. that I knew weren't easy for him to talk about.

One was that R.J. went to a shrink, a Dr. Mendelmann on Park Avenue, twice a week. Seth said he'd been going for two years, since the divorce— that the divorce had been like a roof collapsing on R.J.'s house of problems.

"What kinds of problems?" I asked.

"He's never had many friends, Kitty. He taught himself to read when he was three, but he never allowed himself the luxury of playing . . . having a good time and fooling around like most kids. Dr. Mendelmann's trying to loosen him up. To encourage him to express his feelings. Even to have a good old tantrum if he needs one."

"I'll probably help him make a major breakthrough," I said.

Seth looked at me out of the corner of his eye, smiling. "Yes, in your own way, you're very effective."

Eventually he got around to the subject of Kay. When he said her name, he made it sound sharp like a slap.

"Is she cruel to R.J.?" I asked. "Does she ever lock him in a dark closet or beat him with a broom?"

Seth shook his head. "No, honey, she's not a child abuser. But she's terribly critical of him. Nothing he does satisfies her. He craves her affection, but never gets it."

"Then why don't you have custody of him?"

"I've tried," he said. "I battled with Kay in and

out of court for over two years. But I was traveling a lot in those days—mostly to Europe on different photography assignments. The judge didn't think I could offer R.J. a very stable home life."

"Maybe he'd change his mind if you told him you quit traveling," I said. "Then he'd give you custody."

As soon as the words were out of my mouth, I could have kicked myself. Was I crazy? *I didn't want R.J. living with us!*

I clammed up and looked at Seth. Darn! I'd set him thinking. He was probably going to do just what I suggested—talk to the judge. Then my life would be wrecked. And who would I have to blame? Myself!

Darn! Joy was licking my mitten. She knew how I felt. She's remarkable that way. When I cry, she howls like a wolf, nearly scaring people out of their wits. I can set her off pretending I'm crying. Even talking like I'm sad.

Oh. Oh. Now her head and tail were drooping. I'd have to be careful. I couldn't risk letting her give me away. If Seth guessed I was upset because the last thing I wanted was for him to get custody of R.J., he'd be hurt.

Joy was sniffing my leg. Could she *smell* I was worried? Darn. She could. She was whining.

"She must be cold," Seth said.

"Maybe her little paws are all frostbitten," I said, making my voice as happy and cheerful as possible.

It fooled Joy; she stopped whining. But Seth sure gave me an odd look. And I couldn't let him think I

60

was a horrid person who was happy if her dog was freezing, so I said, "Oh, no . . . I hope they're *not* frostbitten," sounding absolutely heartbroken. "Poor Joy. My poor, poor sweet Joy."

Joy threw her head back, howling, "Waaaaaa-oooooo! Waaaaaaa-ooooooo," as if it were doomsday.

"Maybe we should run the rest of the way and get her in the house fast," I said to Seth, sounding happy and cheerful again.

That perked Joy up. She wagged her tail, waiting for me to make a move, then dashed ahead of Seth and me as we began running. When we caught up with her outside the kitchen door, she had no intention of going inside. She wanted to play and took off like a bullet for our neighbors' yard when their dog barked.

"She's sure acting weird," I said.

I didn't try to coax her back. Seth and I stomped the caked snow off our boots, left them on the mat, then went inside in our stocking feet. My mouth watered as I caught a whiff of the spice cookies cooling on the counter.

From the mess, I knew Sarah had made them. A trail of batter led across the kitchen floor to the phone, where she was holding a wooden spoon, talking. "Oh, shoot, why does it have to be *that* night?" she was saying.

I looked at the cookies. Sarah's never very generous with anything she bakes unless it's burned. These weren't. "You want some?" I said to Seth, not loud enough for her to hear. He nodded, and I scooped a bunch off the cookie sheet.

Sarah was too mad to notice us eating them when she hung up. "Kitty, that was Dad," she said, "and I hope you know we're not going to his house New Year's Eve. We'll be stuck here with a baby sitter."

I asked why, since we're almost always with Dad and Linda on holidays.

"Guess!" she said.

"Because he's on call at the hospital?"

"Yep, and Linda's not feeling good."

Mom had heard Seth and me come in and popped into the kitchen to ask how we'd enjoyed our walk. She smiled at him in a meaningful way as if to say, "Did you and Kitty have your talk?" And he smiled back in a meaningful way as if to say, "Yes, we did," only what he said was, "The woods were breathtaking, Liz."

"And Joy was acting really weird," I added.

"She was probably cold," Mom said. Then she saw Sarah sitting at the counter, moping. "What's the matter, honey? You seem upset."

Sarah told her about New Year's Eve and Mom sighed. "Well, those things happen. And I don't suppose we'll find a baby sitter at this stage . . . It's too late."

I was about to offer my services to sit for Sarah at a cut-rate price, but Seth came up with a better suggestion. "Is there any reason why they can't come to the party with us?" he said to Mom. "My parents would love to see them again."

A party at Mama and Papa's!

Sarah and I threw our arms around each other. "Please?" we begged. "We won't fight going there. We promise."

...6

I doubt if I would have begged to go to the New Year's Eve party if I'd known Seth was bringing R.J. He had to, unfortunately. R.J. was staying overnight with him.

Mama and Papa had an enormous buffet set up. It started on the table in the alcove and ended on two card tables in the hall. And what a feast they'd prepared—everything from potato knishes to noodle pudding to blintzes and meatballs in chafing dishes to a chocolate buttermilk cake you could die for, to little pastries filled with jam.

Their two-bedroom apartment was bursting with old friends and relatives. I recognized Seth's sisters from the pictures I'd seen of them in Mama and Papa's albums. Bernice, the youngest, was visiting from San Francisco. Diane and Enid, the oldest, had come from Connecticut with their husbands and three of

R.J.'s cousins—two girls in high school, and a boy, Andy, who looked a year or two older than R.J. and me.

"What's yellow and slimy and smells like bananas?" Andy asked me when we were introduced.

"What?" I said.

"Monkey barf," he said and laughed.

R.J. seemed anything but thrilled to see Andy. I have to admit that's how I felt. Andy didn't waste a minute telling me he was the family's star jock. He did everything, he claimed. He played soccer, hockey, baseball, ran the fastest quarter mile in his school and just won a second trophy, swimming. I half expected him to pull it out of his pocket and pass it around.

"You wouldn't believe how Kamikaze's growing," he said to R.J. when we lined up at the buffet.

"Who's Kamikaze?" asked Sarah.

"My Doberman," he said without missing a beat before he started burning our ears off about him. "Yeah, he's really terrific . . . You ought to see him," was the windup. "We run three miles together every morning before breakfast."

R.J. kept his eyes lowered, listening quietly as he filled his plate. I thought he looked sad. "Are you still considering sending Kamikaze to obedience school?" he asked Andy.

"Naw. Unless he eats another couch." Andy roared with laughter, scooping up a pile of meatballs. "Say . . . maybe I shouldn't be telling you all this," he said. "I mean I know how your mother won't let you have a pet and all . . . I don't want to make you feel rotten. Did I?"

"I've got a pet. I bought one myself . . . with my own money, yesterday," said R.J.

I was sure that was a big fib.

"Say, terrific," said Andy, sounding very disappointed. "What did you get? A dog?"

R.J. shook his head as if he didn't want to talk about it.

"I bet I know," said Sarah. "You got a snake."

"Yeah, tell us," said Andy.

I watched R.J. bite his lip, wondering what fib he was going to tell next.

"I got a little palomino-colored guinea pig," he said. "I named her Shirley."

"*A guinea pig?*" said Andy.

He had his mouth set to laugh when I noticed Mama eyeing him from the other side of the buffet. "Tell me, darling," she said, cutting him off before he got started, "how's your Spanish tutor working out? Are your grades getting better?"

"A little," said Andy, quickly taking his plate out to the living room.

R.J. followed him in there a minute later, but he was careful not to sit near him. He sat by himself on a hassock, looking miserable until Mom and Bernice asked him to squeeze in between them on the couch.

Sarah and I ate on the floor in a corner with Samantha and Jenny, R.J.'s other cousins. Neither of them were big braggarts like Andy. They told us they lived in a town called Stamford and asked if we were excited about Mom and Seth's wedding. We both said yes without bothering to mention how we felt about R.J.

"We're excited, too," said Samantha. Then she leaned toward us, whispering, "Nobody liked Kay very much . . . She's such a snob. She always thought she was too high class for us."

I couldn't help admiring Samantha's hair. It was short and sassy and fell in a bouncy wave over her cheekbone. Later, when I had to cross through Mama and Papa's bedroom to use the bathroom, I saw a pair of scissors on their dresser. I picked them up, thinking if I shaped my hair a little—trimmed off four or five inches—maybe I could get that cute, sassy look.

Then I decided I'd better not try. If I changed my appearance, R.J. would accuse me of showing off again. I put the scissors back on the dresser, went into the bathroom and combed my hair, leaving it plain and hangdog.

When I finished, I sampled all Mama's cologne atomizers.

She had a collection of them lined up on a shelf above the towel rack. I tried a spritz of each, then a few extra spritzes of the cologne in the green, cut glass bottle. Boy, that was nice. It made my arms and legs smell like gardenias.

When I turned off the light to leave, I heard somebody talking on the phone in the bedroom. It was R.J. I didn't mean to listen in on him, but I couldn't help it. The bathroom door was open a tiny crack.

"Yes, I know you have company, Mom," he was

saying, "and I said I was sorry. I couldn't wait till tomorrow . . . I had to ask you tonight . . . Please change your mind. *Please?* She won't be any . . ."

His mother must have interrupted him midsentence. Either that, or he was crying. After a long silence, he blew his nose, then burst out, "But she *isn't* a filthy rodent! I mean, she's a rodent, but she's clean and she's *domesticated!* . . . Even the Incas had pet guinea pigs! Besides, I promised you I'd take . . ."

Interrupted again. Whew. From what I knew of Kay, she was probably ripping into him. When she finally gave him a chance to say anything, he was so choked up, he could hardly get the words out.

"Well, would you at least hold off until tomorrow?" he begged. *"Please?* I know Dad would keep her for me."

He hung up, then he really let loose. Not loud cries, but little muffled ones like he was burying his face in a pillow so nobody would hear. It didn't matter that I didn't like him much. I felt sorry for him. He really wanted to keep Shirley.

I stood behind the door, breathing with my hand over my mouth. I had to keep quiet. If he had any idea I was in the bathroom, listening, it would be humiliating for both of us. When my legs got tired, I sat on the edge of the tub. His crying didn't seem to be letting up.

It felt like hours had passed before Seth came into the bedroom. "So this is where you've been," he said. "Andy's looking for you. He wants you to play cards with him."

"I don't want to play cards," said R.J.

"Why? What's wrong? Have you been crying?"

R.J. broke up all over again. Between sobs and blowing his nose, he told Seth he had just called Kay. "She's getting rid of Shirley," he said. "I promised I'd take complete responsibility—that I'd clean the cage, feed her . . . do everything. But she's already told the housekeeper she can give Shirley to her nephew."

"Oh, for . . . ! I'll keep Shirley at my place!" Seth said. "I'll pick her up tomorrow."

"She'll be gone, Dad. The housekeeper's taking her home tonight. She's helping Mom with her party."

Without saying a word, Seth stormed across the room, coming down hard on the floor with his heels. "Go tell Liz I'll be out in a few minutes," he said, picking up the phone.

R.J. went out, closing the bedroom door, then I heard Seth dialing. "Mrs. Krampner, please," he said a moment later. While he waited for Kay to come to the phone, I combed my hair in the dark, watching the sparks fly. I stopped when he had Kay on the line.

"Kay, don't waste your time telling me you've got company," he snapped. "I don't care if you're entertaining the queen of England! You're going to listen to what I've got to say!"

I was pretty surprised at how he could lose his temper. He went on, telling Kay off good and loud and I just walked right out of the bathroom, through the bedroom and out the door without him even noticing.

As I passed the kitchen, I saw Mom hand R.J. a wet paper towel. He wiped his face with it, then Mama gave him a tall glass of milk. "Drink, darling," she said, putting the milk container back in the refrigerator. "Calcium will make you feel better."

I was going to keep right on walking by, pretending I hadn't seen them. But Andy came out of the living room, heading down the hall for the kitchen and I wanted to stop him. If he heard the bad news about Shirley, he'd gloat and rub it in more about his Doberman.

"Seen the rabbi anywhere?" he asked me.

I knew he meant R.J. I blocked the kitchen doorway, watching him shuffle a deck of cards. "He's in the kitchen," I said, "but you're not allowed in. He's very, very busy."

"Busy? Why? What's he doing? Eating again?" He peered over my head, looking inside. "Hey, has he been bawling?"

With the partying and singing going on in the living room, I knew it was safe to raise my voice. "Yeah, he has! And it's all your fault, Andy!" I hollered.

He stepped back, staring at me. "*My* fault?"

"That's right! You know what you did."

"I do?"

He looked so guilty I had to think of something to blame on him. "It's because of your dessert," I said.

"My chocolate cake?" he squeaked.

"No, your stupid fork! You left it on a chair and R.J. *sat* on it . . . it gave him four puncture wounds!"

"It did?"

"Yeah, it did . . . and he may need a tetanus shot. Besides that," I said, "you wrecked Mama's good chair! It's got dark chocolate frosting all over it."

"Her light blue chair? The one she just had re-upholstered?" he whispered. "Will it come out?"

"Probably not. So next time take your left-over cake and dirty old utensils out to the kitchen!"

Andy looked as if he wanted to slink away. "You didn't tell Grandma I did it, did you?"

"No, but I will," I said. "I'll rat on you faster than you ever swam in your life if you tell anybody I told you. R.J. doesn't want to make a big thing out of this."

Both of us turned when we heard a door close. Seth was coming out of Mama and Papa's bedroom and Andy glanced nervously from me to him. "I won't tell," he said, quickly. "I swear I won't."

I wanted to change the subject fast. "Bet you a quarter I know a card game you've never heard of," I said, looking at Andy's cards.

"Oh, yeah?" he said, sounding interested. *"What?"*

"Jump-Over-the-Bridge," I said, making up a name.

"Huh?"

Seth fanned the air, whistling as he approached us. "You're sure smelling powerful tonight, Kitty."

"You ought to try standing next to her," said Andy. "She could knock out a horse."

I gave him a dirty look and he cringed. "Listen

. . . I was just joking," he said, "just joking, okay? You smell great! I never smelled a girl who smelled so great."

Seth winked at me, looking amused as he walked by us. He was in a good mood. That meant Kay's housekeeper wasn't taking Shirley home with her.

"If you've got something to tell R.J., he's in the kitchen," I called after him. Then I turned to Andy, sticking out my hand. "Okay. Where's my money? You owe me a quarter."

...7

I didn't see Andy again until March. From New Year's on, however, I saw plenty of R.J.

Kay let him keep Shirley at their apartment. And Shirley was the one subject that could make R.J. smile. If I said, "How's school?" or "Seen any good movies lately?" he'd give me a straight, no-frills answer. But if I said, "How's Shirley doing?" he'd light up and talk for five minutes, telling me what she ate and how many ounces she weighed.

Knowing how he felt about Shirley was the first thing I understood about R.J. To this day I've never let on that I was in Mama and Papa's bathroom, New Year's Eve, listening to him cry over her. I've never told anybody except Minna. I told her the whole story.

She was curious about the same thing I was—what Seth had said to stop Kay from giving Shirley to the housekeeper. "Think he told her he'd knock her teeth out?" she asked me.

I said, "Uh-uh. I don't think he'd talk that rough."

Minna shrugged. "That's what I would have told Kay."

My attitude toward R.J. improved a little after New Year's. Sarah's improved a lot. I think she started liking him, originally, because she discovered he could do a good job helping her with her homework. One time when he came to Briarcliff with Seth he taught her to read a map. Another time he helped her make an Indian village for social studies. They stayed in her room, hours, working on it. I know. I heard them. After that, Sarah looked forward to seeing him. Apparently the feeling was mutual.

Once I asked her what they spent so much time talking about and she said, "Oh, everything," like she knew a dozen interesting things about R.J. that I didn't.

I kept my distance with him. I wasn't friendly or unfriendly. As long as he wasn't telling me I was an exhibitionist, or doing anything irritating, I found I could tolerate him.

I'd had a few weeks of tolerating him when we were invited to Stamford, Connecticut, one afternoon, the beginning of March. Andy's mother had a little get-together for Seth's family. By then, Mom and Sarah and I were considered part of it.

Andy didn't pay much attention to R.J. while we

74

were at his house, except to corner him to watch how high Kamikaze could leap after a doggie donut. "Bet your guinea pig can't do that," he said.

"No, she can't," R.J. said without apologizing for her.

I got the royal treatment. Andy showed me his chin-up bar and weight-lifting apparatus in the basement, then took me upstairs to his room to see his swimming trophies. "Say, you never told Grandma I got frosting on her good chair, did you?" he whispered on the way.

"Never mentioned it," I said.

"Hey, you're okay, cuz," he said, giving me an old-buddy whack on the back.

"*Cuz?*"

"Sure. We're almost cousins, aren't we?"

I knew he wanted something; he was pouring it on too thick. He kept me in suspense until I'd seen his trophies and new soccer shoes. Then he pulled a deck of cards out of his pocket. "You know that game, Jump-Over-the-Bridge, you told me about on New Year's Eve?"

"Yeah, what about it?" I said.

"Well, I won a buck-fifty in bets off it. But now my friends are after me to teach it to them. If I don't, they'll think I made the name up."

I acted surprised. "Really?"

"Yeah! Can you believe that?" he said, sounding peeved.

I let him think he'd conned me into teaching him how to play, and we played five games of Jump-Over-the-Bridge, betting a quarter a game. Of course I didn't know what I was doing any more than he did. I had to make it up as we went along.

It turned into sort of a mixture of Crazy Eights, Fish and Hearts. And since I could invent new rules whenever I felt like it, I took advantage of the sevens, jacks and aces I kept drawing. I made the sevens and jacks wild and the aces worth a thousand points each. Then I told Andy his kings and queens counted against him.

He seemed a little confused at times, but I don't think it bothered him that I won all five games. He paid me on the spot. "Here's your buck and a quarter," he said like he was grateful to be giving it to me.

When it was time to leave, he walked me out to Seth's car to say goodbye. I doubt if he would have remembered to say anything to R.J. or Sarah if his mother hadn't reminded him.

" 'Bye," he said to please her, then he watched me climb into the back seat. "See you at the wedding, cuz," he called as we drove off.

R.J. brooded like he was upset almost all the way to Briarcliff. I thought it was probably because Sarah had fallen asleep with her head on his shoulder and her hair smelled bad. But I noticed he kept eyeing me. Finally he said, "You and Andy really like each other, don't you, Kitty?"

"Not especially," I said.

"You certainly had fun playing cards . . . I saw you."

"That's because I was making the game up," I said.

He looked at me as if he didn't believe me and that irritated me so much, I didn't say another word to him. I concentrated on a little bump over my eyebrow. It itched like crazy.

That night I was covered with itchy bumps. I had chicken pox. Ten days later, Sarah got them. She was sicker than I'd been and stayed out of school longer. Every day that she was home, R.J. called her.

While she was still in her scab stage, Mom sold our house to some people who had seen it several times since it was put on the market in January. They wanted to move in by the end of June and Mom agreed to have us out by then. But it didn't give us much time. She and Seth had to start a frantic search for a loft in Soho.

When they weren't looking, they were working. Mom had four book jackets to finish before the wedding, and Set had to develop the photographs for a book on Colonial inns. As a result, Sarah and I spent more time than usual with Dad and Linda in Croton.

Besides staying with them on weekends, we had dinner at their house two or three times a week all spring. That was a treat for us because we got a chance to see more of Peter and Sylvia. We fixed them super-duper bubble baths with foot-high foam and read them bedtime stories. When Peter's first tooth came out, Linda said we could be the Tooth Fairy.

I wrote him a note from the Tooth Fairy, saying

she'd heard about his tooth while she was in China and had flapped her wings all day to get to Croton. She was sorry he was asleep. But if he looked around his room, he'd find the money she left for him. It was a dollar's worth of dimes that Sarah had hidden under his pillow and inside his toy box.

One night during spring vacation, Linda and Dad told the four of us they had some marvelous news—Linda was pregnant. At the end of September, we were going to have a baby brother or sister.

When Sarah and I went home the next day, we felt kind of funny breaking the news to Mom. We weren't sure how she would take it. Sarah thought she might think Dad had no business being anybody's father except ours. I thought she might not want us to have a brother or sister who wasn't related to her.

We were relieved that Mom didn't have either reaction. She said she was very happy for Dad and Linda. And she really sounded like she meant it.

The next person I told about the baby was Minna.

The next person Sarah told was R.J.

His private school in the city was having spring vacation the same time our school in Briarcliff was. Toward the end of the week he came to spend an afternoon with us while Mom and Seth went to see the caterers about the wedding.

"R.J., you'll never guess the good, good, good news," Sarah said as she ushered him into the house.

"Linda's pregnant . . . We're getting a baby brother or sister."

R.J. got so excited, it annoyed me. "I'd like to remind you that it's not *your* brother or sister," I said.

"I'm aware of that," he said, "but I still feel a little related."

While I stayed in the TV room watching a boring soap opera by myself, he and Sarah decided to think of names for the baby. I heard them going through bookcases all over the house, looking for ideas.

"How about Huckleberry?" called Sarah.

"It doesn't go well with Birdsall," R.J. answered.

"Would Wilbur or Charlotte?"

"Yes, but people would know where you got them."

Eventually they agreed on putting her in charge of a list of girls' names and him in charge of a list for boys. When they came into the TV room, interrupting my program to read them to me, I told them I didn't like any name on either list. "Especially Pippi and Ramona," I said, knowing they were Sarah's suggestions.

"What if I'd written down Charlotte?" she asked.

I pulled a face. "Ewww, no! It sounds like a spider."

"You rotten crab . . . You spoil everything fun!" she said, wadding her list of names to throw at me.

The paper hit me on the nose. I could hardly feel it, but I jumped up and down, screaming, to scare her anyway, and threatened to tell Mom and Seth when they came back from the caterers'. "You saw her throw it at me," I said to R.J. "She started this."

He didn't say anything. He never does when we have fights. He just keeps quiet and acts superior, which drives me up the wall.

"My whole face throbs," I cried, watching to see if he would take my side. "It's killing me . . . absolutely killing me! Look . . . I can hardly move my mouth!"

Without a word, he folded his list of boys' names and stuck it in his pocket. "Kitty, maybe if you were distracted you'd forget about it," he said.

I was ready to yell, "Oh, no, I wouldn't," when I heard quick, short blasts coming from the doorbell. Somebody was jabbing impatiently at it. I ran to answer it and found Minna hopping up and down with a big, brown bag.

"It's full of jellybeans," she squealed as I opened the door for her. "I won them . . . The deli had a contest and I guessed eighteen hundred seventy-nine. . ."

"How many are there?"

"Eighteen hundred eighty-four!"

"What deli?" said Sarah, who'd run to the door behind me.

"Danny's . . . where my mom buys bagels! They just called twenty minutes ago!"

We hurried Minna into the living room and watched her dump a load of jellybeans on the coffee table. "Everybody grab ten," she screamed. "You, too, R.J. . . . Dive in!"

I grabbed mine as Minna flopped on the couch,

trying to catch her breath. "Mom says I have to share . . . but I was going to anyway. Wow! Can you believe it," she said, popping off the couch to shower the floor with the rest of the jellybeans. "Eighteen hundred and eighty-four!"

It was a sight I'll never forget. I raced upstairs to get my camera and by the time I got downstairs again, Minna had organized a jellybean hunt. Even R.J. was running around, helping her and Sarah hide them. "Now what we'll do," she said, "is eat every red one we find, and when we come across a green one, we'll yell 'stop'! Then we'll all switch shoes."

I can't remember ever having more fun. When Mom and Seth came home from the caterers', we were all whooping it up, tossing jellybeans back and forth to see how many we could catch with our mouths. None of us heard the door open, but Mom heard us.

"Is everything all right?" she hollered over the zinging and pinging of jellybeans.

I won't deny the place was a mess. To get to the jellybeans we'd scattered underneath tables, behind the curtains and down inside the crevices of the couch, we practically had to disassemble the whole room.

Mom didn't seem to notice. She and Seth were watching R.J. clomp around in my red sneakers, looking sweaty and slovenly. Normally he has to be in a car accident just to get his hair mussed.

I knew *exactly* what they were thinking: *"Wouldn't Dr. Mendelmann be pleased to see this?"*

"Looks as if you've been having a good time," said Seth.

R.J. nodded with his cheeks puffed.

"Well, you kids go right on playing," said Mom. "Seth and I are going to be outside, looking at the yard."

There were hundreds and hundreds of jelly-beans left that we hadn't eaten. I gave everybody plastic freezer bags and we started collecting the ones we'd hidden in hard-to-find places.

"I just *knew* something good was going to happen this week," Minna said as she reached for a jellybean under the fireplace grate. "My horoscope said I'd soar to surprising heights in my high cycle."

"You believe in horoscopes?" asked R.J.

"Oh, definitely. They're one hundred percent accurate if you read them right," said Minna. "Don't you follow yours?"

"He doesn't have to," cut in Sarah. "He can tell his fortune any time he wants with his very own special fortune-telling cards."

Minna sat back on her heels, impressed. *"You can, R.J.?* Kitty never told me."

"That's because he never told *me,*" I said, annoyed that he'd only told Sarah. "What do your cards look like, R.J.? . . . And don't you *dare* tell me, Sarah!"

"They're hand-painted, antique ivory tarot cards," he said. "I bought them at an auction."

"Since *when* can kids bid at auctions?" said Minna.

R.J. shrugged. "Maybe they can't at some, but the one where I go lets me . . . They know my grandfather," he said. "They've been cashing my birthday checks from him for the last three years."

"Papa sends you birthday checks?" I said, hoping I'd get one.

"No, my mother's father does."

"Were the tarot cards expensive?" asked Minna.

"Sort of," he said.

"How expensive?"

He hedged a second. "Well, they're not just cards for amusement. They're also an art investment."

"*How* much?" she pressed.

"None of your big, fat business, Minna," yelled Sarah. "If R.J. doesn't want to tell you, he doesn't have to."

That made me mad. I couldn't see a thing wrong with Minna's question. I'm always asking people how much they've paid for things. And so is Sarah. "You don't have to be so snippy!" I told her.

"And you don't have to be so nosy," she yelled back.

I turned to Minna. "Come, dear," I said, trying to sound very dignified. "If you and I are to be treated so discourteously, we shall have to depart."

She tossed her head the way I had. "But, of course. Shall we go to thy chamber?"

"Divine idea," I said, pressing my freezer bag of jellybeans against my bosom.

We walked slowly, arm in arm, past R.J. and Sarah, holding our noses in the air. "Don't they make you sick?" Sarah said to him as we started up the stairs.

Minna didn't say anything to me until we were

out of sight at the landing. "Betcha I know how much he paid for his cards," she whispered.

I looked at her. "Really? How much?"

"Ten dollars."

"Because they're ivory?"

"Uh-uh. Because he cashed his birthday check for them."

"It could have been a check for five," I said.

Minna shook her head. "Not if it was from his grandfather. Relatives always send ten. Every year that's what my grandmother sends me."

Neither of us knew I had something in my jelly-bean bag that would lead us to the actual amount he had paid for his cards. It was a little piece of paper, folded several times, that was stuck to a smooshed green jellybean. When I noticed it later, I threw it in my wastebasket, thinking it was nothing more than R.J.'s list of boys' names.

By that time, R.J. had already gone back to the city with Seth in order to keep a late afternoon doctor's appointment.

I think that's when he realized something was missing . . .

...8

Minna slept over that night and we watched a wonderful movie on Home Box Office. It was about an American guy who was knocked unconscious in a horrible train wreck in Austria. He woke up in a hospital in the Alps, not knowing a word of German, or who he was. He'd been stricken with amnesia.

Sarah fell asleep just before he had a love affair with the beautiful blonde nurse who called him Hans. But Minna and I watched till the very end when Hans remembered he was really Charlie Bugle from Chicago. He had to say goodbye to the nurse and go home to his wife.

It was so sad we both cried.

We were lying in bed, eating jellybeans, still talking about the movie when the phone rang. I heard Mom answer it in the hall. I thought it was probably Seth calling, but Mom tapped on my door to tell me it was R.J. "Honey, he's sorry it's so late. But he says it's very important."

I yawned, pretending I'd been in a deep sleep, when I said hello.

"Kitty, have you seen a little piece of paper I lost," he said, ignoring my yawn. "It's folded so it's no bigger than a matchbook."

"Is it your list of boys' names?" I asked.

"No, I've got that," he said. "The paper I'm looking for is *extremely* personal . . . a doctor I go to asked me to write it. It must've fallen out of my pocket during the jellybean hunt."

I told him it was probably the paper stuck to the jellybean that I'd thrown in my wastebasket. "But I can still dig it out," I said.

"No, don't! Please don't!" he said, sounding panicked.

"I thought you needed it."

"I'll write another one."

"Then why did you wake me up?" I snapped.

"I just wanted to make *sure* I lost it before I wrote another one."

"Don't try and fool me," I said. "You thought if I found it, I'd read it. Admit it!"

"Please promise you won't touch it," he begged.

I promised and stomped back to my room, mad at myself. As much as I wanted to take it out of my wastebasket, I couldn't. I have a thing about promises. I have to keep them or I feel guilty.

"What's wrong?" Minna said when I closed the door.

"You know the paper stuck to that icky jellybean in my bag?"

"Yeah, you threw it out . . . I saw you."

"Well, it's something *extremely* personal that R.J. wrote for the shrink he goes to," I said, getting into bed. "He made me promise I wouldn't touch it, so now I can't dig it out to read it!"

"Sure you can."

"No, I can't, Minna! You know how I am about promises."

"You didn't promise him that *I* wouldn't take it out of your wastebasket, did you?"

"No." She had a very good point. It started me thinking. "I guess it's okay if you dig it out," I said.

The paper had slipped down near the bottom of the wastebasket under a black banana peel and a Sugar Daddy stick. Minna had to wipe it off with a tissue and pick off the jellybean. I was very careful not to break my promise. I didn't touch it.

"Boy, he sure likes to fold things tiny," Minna said. Then she groaned. "Hey, he wrote *this* for his shrink? *A list of school supplies?* . . 2 gum erasers, 1 spiral notebook, a box of #2 lead, Empire pencils . . ."

The paper R.J. was really worried about was under a couch cushion down in the living room. It took Minna and me fifteen minutes, creeping around with a flashlight, before we found it. I saw it first, but she picked it up.

"This had better be it," I said. "We've gone to a lot of trouble."

Mom's door was still closed when we got upstairs. She hadn't heard us. Neither had Joy. She was sleeping on the bathroom rug.

"Some watchdog," said Minna. "It's a good thing we're not burglars."

We hurried back to my room with the folded paper; apparently R.J. folds everything. "Yeah, this is it. It's a list of his goals," Minna said as she smoothed it flat on my bedspread.

I sat next to her and we read it together:

My Short-Range Goals	*My Long-Range Goals*
1. Analyze why Kitty doesn't like me.	*1. Improve my personality (a) smile more (b) tell jokes (c) learn to be more assertive.*
2. Get away from my mother this summer.	
3. Find a sleep-away camp that doesn't believe in competitive sports.	*2. Overcome my phobias.*
	3. Try to understand why mother is the kind of person she is.
4. Read a book on Indo-China.	*4. Stop being self-conscious about (a) my art investments (b) the Lerner family's money (c) my trust fund.*
5. For fun: learn to swivel peel an orange like the waiters at the Waldorf.	
	5. Achieve #'s 1–4 so I can stop my psychoanalysis.

We read and reread what R.J. had written.

Neither of us could figure out what swivel peeling an orange meant or why he'd think it was fun.

"But I can understand why he wants to improve his personality," said Minna.

"Yeah, so can I. He looks better when he smiles," I said. "But I don't think he should waste time trying to analyze why I don't like him. He should just ask me. I'd tell him."

Parts (b) and (c) under number four in R.J.'s list of long-range goals stumped us the most. "What's a trust fund?" I asked Minna.

She took a guess. "I think it's money parents make kids put in the bank for things like college. I must have one. My dad always makes me save my birthday checks."

"Why would R.J. be self-conscious about his?"

"If he blows his birthday checks on art investments, maybe he doesn't have much money in it."

That made sense. Now if we could only figure out who the Lerners were. "Maybe they're some rich kids who go to R.J.'s private school," I said.

"Has he ever mentioned them?"

"Not to me he hasn't."

"What about to Sarah?"

"If he has, she'd never tell us," I said.

Minna thought a minute. "You want to try an experiment on Sarah?"

"Stick her hand in warm water?"

"Uh-uh. Get her to talk in her sleep. A guy I once saw on a TV science program said it works like truth serum on some people. The right types will tell you things they never would awake."

"Let's go," I said.

Sarah was sound asleep, clutching Flossie, her battered old pink rabbit, when we tiptoed into her room. As we passed her dresser, inching our way toward her bed, we heard little gag-a-gack snoring noises. One ended with a whistle that doubled us over. "That came from her nose," Minna whispered.

"Dad says she's got big adenoids," I said.

Both of us giggled when we got close enough to see Sarah's face. "Look at her mouth!" said Minna. It was wide open and I draped one of Flossie's ears across Sarah's upper lip so she looked like she had a mustache. That just killed us.

Minna gave herself a finger mustache. Then I gave myself one. Then we started going, "gag-a-gack, gag-a-gack" every time Sarah did until we fell all over each other, laughing.

Sarah kept right on sleeping. She didn't miss a mini-snore. After we quieted down enough to get on with our business, we knelt beside her bed.

"Sarahhh," Minna whispered in a spooky voice. "Tell us the tru-uuth! Whooo are the Lerners? What do you know about their moneyyy?"

We held our breath and waited. And waited. And waited.

"Think I should try saying it a little closer to her?" Minna whispered. I nodded and she leaned over, cupping her hands around Sarah's ear as if she were ready to holler through a tunnel. "Sarahh, you must tell us the tru-uuth! Whooo are the Lerners? What do you know about their moneyyy?"

Sarah's eyes flew open and she bolted upright,

hugging Flossie to her chest. *"What money?"* she called out. *"Who said that?"*

Minna and I flung ourselves down on her rug before she could see us. "I-I-I did," Minna continued. "I'mmm a ghoooost and I demand to know about the Lerner's moneyyyy!"

"Baloney you're a ghost, Minna! I know your dumb voice." Sarah's mattress springs squeaked as she bounced to the edge of her bed. "I see you and Kitty down there. And I'm not telling you one thing about R.J.'s grandfather's money!"

"You mean his *rich* Grandfather Lerner's money?" I said.

"That's right. So get out of here."

"We'll make you a deal," said Minna. "If you tell us how big R.J.'s trust fund is, we'll tell you how much he paid for his tarot cards."

"Burn on you, Minna! He told me how much he paid for his cards weeks ago."

"No, he didn't."

"Yes, he did."

"Then prove it," I said. "Tell us how big his birthday check was."

Sarah reached for the circus flashlight she keeps under her pillow and flashed it in my face. "You think you can trick me, Kitty. But you can't! His grandfather sent him a blank check."

"So he could write in the exact amount he bid?" asked Minna.

"Maybe. And maybe not," said Sarah. "I wouldn't tell you if you tortured me."

"We already know his grandfather won't let him bid higher than ten dollars," I said.

Sarah was getting annoyed. "You don't know anything! His grandfather wants him to have *good* art investments . . . He lets him bid twenty times that much!"

"You mean he paid *two hundred dollars* for his tarot cards?" I said.

"Who told you?" she screamed.

Minna and I hurried out of her room and back into mine, hopping into bed fast so we could pretend we were asleep if Mom came in. When there was no sign of her, Minna rolled over, facing me.

"I wouldn't be self-conscious if my mother's family was rich, would you?" she whispered.

"No, I'd tell everybody," I said.

"Same with me. Do you think R.J. is afraid kids will think he's spoiled and tease him?"

I'd been lying there wondering the same thing. "Uh-uh. I think it's something else," I said. "I think he just wants to be a regular kid."

"Don't you think a kid can be rich *and* regular?"

"Sure. But I don't think he does."

"Maybe we can help him," she said.

...9

I didn't think R.J.'s chances of becoming a regular kid looked very promising when I saw him in New York the next day. He carried on something fierce over riding in a freight elevator.

Neither of us had known we would be seeing each other so soon.

I had planned on spending the day making macaroni jewelry with Minna, Mom had planned on working on a book jacket at home and Sarah had planned on going bike riding with her friend Jamie.

A quick call from Seth after breakfast changed everybody's plans. Mom jotted down an address he gave her and by ten, she had Sarah and me in our car, racing into the city. We were going to see a loft in Soho.

"What's supposed to be so great about it?" I asked.

"It's got high ceilings, huge windows and it's

within our price range," Mom said. "Seth thinks it was made to order for us."

"Is R.J. coming?"

"Yes, I'm sure he is. He stayed over with Seth last night."

I picked at my nail, waiting for Sarah to spill the beans about the ghosts who'd visited her during the night. I'd been waiting all morning. Why wasn't she saying anything?

"How'd you sleep?" I asked her, thinking it was better to have it out with her now, rather than in front of R.J.

She looked at me, blankly. "I slept fine."

I couldn't believe it; she'd forgotten. She must have gone right back to sleep as soon as Minna and I ran out of her room. In a way, it was almost disappointing.

I slumped down in the car seat and began asking Mom more questions about the loft. Was it big? She said it was—thirty-two hundred square feet of raw space on the fifth floor of an old shoe factory.

"But you shouldn't be put off by the fact that the building is an old factory," she added. "It's being converted into family co-ops with two lofts on each floor. The one we're going to see is the only loft that hasn't been sold."

Seth had looked at it early in the morning with a real estate agent and thought it had "wonderful possibilities."

"I think this is it, Liz," he said when we met him and R.J. in front of the building's entrance.

I looked at the workmen sandblasting the grimy, gray exterior. A factory is a factory no matter how clean it is, I thought. And I didn't want to live in one. I didn't like the iron grilles on the ground-floor windows. And I hated the crouching gargoyles on the ugly brown brick building across the street.

"Those things would give me nightmares for sure," I said.

"But they're copies of the ones on Notre Dame Cathedral in Paris," R.J. said as if that made them all right.

I didn't like the suspicious way he was eyeing me when we went up the steps. I knew he was wondering if I'd dug through my wastebasket for the paper he'd lost. Wouldn't he be surprised if I told him it was nothing but a list of school supplies?

"Did you keep your promise?" he whispered.

"Yes, of course I did," I said, which was the gospel truth. But for some reason I didn't feel right saying it.

He was still eyeing me, trying to decide if he should believe me and I pretended I was interested in what Seth was telling Mom about some architectural details above the door. "You mean those little gizmos up there are cast-*iron?*" I said like I cared.

Seth smiled. "They sure are . . . so is the entire ceiling in the lobby. It's a beauty."

Then he opened the door and we all filed into a place that looked like a mile-high cave. *This is a lobby,* I thought. It was dingier than our basement crawl space.

Two feet from the door I felt dust coating my teeth and braces. It was thick and gritty and most of it was coming from the corner where a guy was working with a pneumatic drill. Diagonally across from him, two plumbers were tearing out an old steam radiator. Smack in the center of this cavelike place was a towering scaffold. Several workmen were on the top, scraping green paint off a domed ceiling twenty feet above our heads.

Seth motioned for us to walk around the scaffold and I saw Mom look up, admiring the waffle design that was beginning to emerge from under the green paint. "You're right, honey . . . It is a beauty," she said to Seth.

"Baloney it is," said Sarah. "It looks like the bottoms of my sneakers."

I was definitely against the building. If we were going to live in the city, I wanted a sleek, modern lobby with mirrors and a desk and a concierge who could take secret messages for me and put them in one of those interesting pigeonholes like you see in movies.

The dust had put me in a very bad mood. "Where's the elevator?" I yelled over the drill.

Seth heard me. He stopped inspecting a cast-iron pillar long enough to tell me the elevator was around the corner and down the hall to my left. "But you'll have to wait for the real estate agent," he said. "He's upstairs showing the loft to some other people. He'll be down in a minute."

It was closer to five minutes before the real estate agent came. He was a Mr. Jaffe from Butler and

Ballard Associates. And I was glad he was one of those fast-talking, rude New Yorkers who lets you know right off he can't stand kids. He'd rather spit in your eye than talk about architectural details. That suited me. I didn't want to talk about them, either.

Mr. Jaffe took us straight to the elevator.

R.J. nearly collapsed when he saw it. But I was kind of fascinated. It was an early model freight elevator the size of a small school bus. The top was wide open so you could look up at the cables. And the sides were ribbed like a cage, covered with see-through steel mesh so you could look down the shaft.

I stepped right in behind Mr. Jaffe. Then I noticed no one else was coming. Mom, Seth and Sarah were still in the hall talking to R.J., who had broken out in a sweat. "I'm not riding in it!" he said, backing up against the wall as if he were ready to claw his way out of the building. "I'm not!"

"Of course you are!" said Mr. Jaffe. "How do you expect to live in New York if you're afraid of elevators?"

"He already lives in New York . . . in a *luxury* building," said Sarah.

Mr. Jaffe gave her a dirty look and she shot him one back. "Are you coming now?" he said to R.J.

R.J. shook his head, refusing to move. Watching him made me realize he hadn't made much progress in overcoming his phobias.

"The elevator's safe, R.J. . . . really it is," said Seth. "I rode in it earlier. It just passed an inspection last month."

Mr. Jaffe sighed. "Of course it's safe!"

"Not to somebody who's afraid of heights like he is," said Sarah. She sounded almost sweet, maybe even motherly. Then she took R.J.'s hand and slipped it between hers. "R.J., if you'd feel better walking upstairs, I'll walk up with you."

R.J. bit his lip and swallowed. "Okay."

Mom volunteered to walk up with them, then Seth said he would, so Mom came with me. She was stony silent until Mr. Jaffe stopped the elevator on the fifth floor.

"Mr. Jaffe," she said coldly, as we stepped out, "we are *not* here to waste your time. We're here to buy a loft! But we won't consider this building unless we know a new elevator is going to be installed."

Mr. Jaffe did a double take. "Why, yes . . . there will be one, actually. In September," he said.

From then on, his attitude toward us changed. He was pleasant. He waited by the stairwell with Mom and me, and when Seth came up with R.J. and Sarah, he apologized to all of us for seeming impatient.

"I guess I've gotten too mechanical about this," he said. "But in the last six weeks I've shown the building to over a thousand people. A good ninety percent of them just came to amuse themselves during their lunch hours." He sighed and reached in his pocket for a key. "A guy, yesterday, stuck his sour pickle in my briefcase."

Mom and Seth laughed, which brought a limp smile to Mr. Jaffe's face. "Here, son," he said, handing his key to R.J. "You can open the door if you want. It's the loft on the left."

"Who bought the loft across from it?" asked Sarah.

"A sculptor by the name of Aaron Lebowitz, his lovely wife Michiko . . ."

"Michiko?" I said.

"Yes, she's Japanese . . . You ought to see the origami flowers she makes," said Mr. Jaffe, "and of course, their seven children," he added very quickly.

"Oh, good, seven kids," said Sarah. "They must have some girls."

The rest is history. We bought the loft. To me, it was a big, empty, nondescript nothing with ceilings, a floor and a tangle of pipes in every corner. No walls, no kitchen, no bathrooms, no anything and no promise of anything unless it was flooded, then frozen and turned into an ice-skating rink.

But Mom and Seth loved it. They saw no end to what a little imagination could do. One of them would say, "Honey, can't you just imagine this expanse over here left open so it's flooded with light?" Then the other one would say, "That's just what I was thinking."

They were thinking alike at every corner and in between. And less than forty-five minutes later, they left a deposit.

Loft 5-B at 16 Greene Street in Soho in New York City was ours.

...10

The reality of moving away from Briarcliff really hit me after I'd seen the loft. Raw space seemed like a crazy exchange for a nice, comfortable two-story red brick house with an acre of lawn and a birdbath.

Whenever I crabbed about it to Mom, she'd laugh and tell me. "Oh, honey, you wait . . . When the loft is finished, it'll be a knockout. You'll love it."

She and Seth scarcely wasted a minute hiring an architect to draw up plans for the renovations. By the middle of April he had blueprints to show us. All the blue lines and hieroglyphics meant that thirty-two hundred square feet of nothing was going to be transformed, hocus-pocus, into nine wonderful rooms, not counting two bathrooms and a darkroom for Seth.

Of course, none of this magic was going to take place overnight. An army of workmen would need several months to do it. That meant the loft wouldn't be ready when we moved in at the end of June. Some of the walls would be up for privacy and we would have electricity, but not much else. Not even a place to cook unless we used a hot plate.

"We'll turn that inconvenience into something positive," Seth promised. "We'll have fun all summer discovering little neighborhood cafes in Soho."

The Big Date wasn't far off. The wedding was set for May twenty-seventh and we had a lot to do.

Flowers and bouquets were ordered. A portable organ was reserved for the twenty-seventh and an organist was hired to play it. Mom took Sarah and me shopping for our dresses, then sometime in early May, three men from the catering service came to our house to map out the backyard. Since Mom and Seth had decided to exchange vows outdoors, under our weeping willow tree, the caterers had to plan in advance where to set up chairs for fifty guests.

The day they came, Seth drove up to Briarcliff with R.J. Sarah, Minna and I couldn't wait till they got there. R.J. was bringing something special—his tarot cards. He had promised to tell us our fortunes.

Mine was a terrible disappointment.

So were R.J.'s fancy-schmancy two hundred dollar, ivory cards. They were over three hundred years old and as chipped and yellow as Joy's back teeth. The paintings on them weren't very good, either. In my opinion, artists back in the seventeenth century couldn't draw kids nearly as well as someone modern like Norman Rockwell. The bodies were too long, even on babies, and the heads were too small. None of the women had decent eyebrows. "That's why I've always hated the Mona Lisa," I said to R.J.

He couldn't have been more shocked. "But, Kitty, Leonardo da Vinci was one of the world's greatest artists! His Mona Lisa is a masterpiece."

"Not to me," I said. "She's greenish and she looks sick and oily. I like the pink-cheeked girls with the long eyelashes in the Breck Shampoo ads."

He didn't argue. He went ahead and set his yellow, chipped cards in special stacks for fortune-telling, arranging them in the shape of the letter H. Then he began telling our fortunes.

Each of us had a card drawn that was supposed to be more significant than the others:

Sarah's significant card had a painting of three maidens with golden goblets, dancing in a flower garden.

Minna's had a high priestess sitting on an elegant throne, holding an important scroll in her lap.

Mine had two ragged, hunched-over beggars walking barefoot through a snowstorm at night.

Before R.J. bothered explaining what it meant, I knew I didn't want it. I told him to go ahead and draw me another significant card.

"But I can't," he said. "That's not the way this is done." Then he went into a long spiel, telling me the pictures were only symbols—that I shouldn't take them too seriously. "All your card means is that

102

you're going to have some temporary disorder and chaos in your life."

Right then and there, I dared him to draw *his* most significant card. He did, and when he saw it, he didn't seem much happier than I'd been with mine. To me it was okay. It just had a big, powerful fist thrust through a cloud, grasping a stick.

"Does it mean you'll grow up to be a fighter?" I asked.

He shook his head. "Uh-uh. That's a wand, not a stick."

"What does the wand mean?"

"Oh, not much. Just something about money."

"What *kind* of money?" said Minna.

R.J. shrugged. "Money's money, isn't it? I guess it means I'm supposed to inherit some, someday."

I felt Minna nudge me. For weeks we'd been waiting for this moment. We wanted to let him know it was a crying shame he didn't appreciate being rich. Now was perfect. We could bring it up so naturally he wouldn't realize we had read his list of goals or knew about the Lerners.

"I sure wish that had been *my* card," I said.

"Same with me," said Minna. "I *love* money. I go around feeling embarrassed to death all the time because nobody in my family has any."

"You do?" said Sarah. "I didn't know that."

Minna nodded. "Oh, yes. I'm awfully self-conscious about it."

"You are?" This was all coming as a total surprise to Sarah. "Are you very poor, Minna?"

"Very. I hardly have any money in my trust fund."

"I don't even have a trust fund," I said. "And I think people who inherit money should be very, very proud of themselves."

R.J. seemed terribly disturbed by what we were saying. "You and Minna are both wrong to feel that way," he said. "It's much better when people work and earn their own money."

"Give us one good reason," said Minna.

"It builds character. Getting money too easily spoils some people."

"Who for instance?"

"Like a certain woman I know," he said. "She's been manipulating other people all her life because her family's rich."

"Did you ever stop to think she might have been that way even if her family was poor?" said Minna.

R.J. started putting his tarot cards back in their velvet-lined leather case. "No, I guess I haven't."

After Minna went home, Mom asked Sarah to set the table and me to put some dirty clothes in the washer and fold what was in the dryer. It's a job I hate, so I didn't turn R.J. down when he offered to come down to the basement to help me. He said he'd had a lot of experience helping his mother's house-keeper when her back went out. But I had a feeling he just wanted to talk.

He was quiet until I poured the detergent into

the washer. Then he said, "You know, Kitty, I think my dad and your mom are going to have an excellent marriage."

I set the timer and closed the lid. "So do I."

"They really love each other."

"Yes, I know . . . very much."

"And they never argue," he said.

Both of us loaded the clothes from the dryer onto the laundry table and started folding. I watched him pick up a towel and make perfect creases in it like it was the American flag. "Did your parents fight much when they were married?" I asked.

"Yes, constantly. What about yours?"

"Usually they stopped talking to each other," I said. "Dad ignored Mom and she slept on the couch. But the divorce made them friends again."

He laid the towel in the laundry basket and picked up a pair of socks. "Mine still argue."

"Why? They're not living together."

"They argue over me mostly," he said. "And my mother's the instigator. She likes being in complete control." He rolled up the socks and reached for a T-shirt. "She's never loved me much."

"Oh, sure she does, R.J. All mothers love their children."

He shook his head. "No, not always, Kitty. Sometimes I think she just wanted custody of me to hurt Dad."

I was struggling with one of Sarah's tangled Peanut's sheets, dragging most of it on the floor, and he put down the T-shirt to help me. "Remember earlier when I mentioned a woman who manipulated people?" he said as he brought his end of the sheet up to meet mine.

I nodded.

"Well, the woman I was talking about is my mother."

We were face to face over the half-folded sheet. I knew he hadn't made that confession just to let me know his mother was rich. Something was bothering him.

"What exactly does your mother do?" I asked.

"She has a certain kind of attitude," he said. "She expects to get whatever she wants. If she doesn't get something automatically, she tries charm. If that doesn't work, she pulls strings."

"Pulls strings?"

"You know . . . uses her money. Her influence. Dad saw right through her. That's why he left her and . . ." He hesitated, looking at me as if he wasn't sure he should go on. Then he said, "Maybe you already know this, Kitty, but I went to a psychiatrist for a couple of years . . . a Dr. Mendelmann. We used to discuss how I felt about these things."

I picked up on the word "went." "You're not going any more?"

"No, I stopped. My mother called him three weeks ago and told him I was quitting."

"Because you wanted to?"

"Uh-uh. Because she wanted me to. She thought he was turning me against her. But he wasn't really. He was trying to help me understand her."

106

I still couldn't figure out why he had suddenly decided to confide so much. What was he leading up to? First he talked about the wedding. Then he switched to his mother. How were they connected?

"Is your mother mad that my mom's going to be the next Mrs. Seth Krampner?" I asked.

He shrugged. "I don't know. She's never said."

I tried another approach. "Would she ever try to manipulate my mom?" Oh, oh, I thought. He has a funny look on his face. "*Would she, R.J.?*"

"Not directly."

"How then?"

"I'm not sure exactly. It's just that . . . Well, she's been making a lot of transatlantic phone calls lately. To London."

"What for? Did she tell you?"

"No . . . She's very secretive. And yesterday I saw a registered letter on her desk. It was from the headmaster of an English school. The Lathrop Boys Academy it was called. Now I'm worried that she's planning on moving over there."

"Can't you come right out and ask her?"

He seemed puzzled. "Ask her?"

"Yeah, you know. Have a fit and say, 'Hey, look, Mom! I'm getting sick and tired of you sneaking around. Are we moving to London, or aren't we?' Like that."

R.J. cringed. "You don't know her," he said. "If she has a reason for not telling me, she won't."

"What if you threatened to run away?"

"She doesn't fall for hysteria."

I was running out of suggestions. "Well, what's your dad doing? . . . Is he making a big court case out of this? I know mine would. He'd be madder than blazes if Mom ever tried sneaking Sarah and me to London."

R.J. bit his lip.

"You mean you haven't told him?" I said.

"I can't, Kitty . . . Not now. The wedding is only three weeks away."

"So?"

He didn't say anything.

We were still clinging to the sheet, keeping it raised above our feet like it was a steel curtain. My arms were getting tired. I wanted to drop the darn thing, and I started to . . . then it hit me! R.J. hadn't told Seth because a big court battle would spoil the wedding! Maybe even postpone it!

Now I was scared. May twenty-seventh had to be a beautiful day. I was going to be a flower girl. Upstairs in my closet was a gorgeous pale lavender dress that matched Sarah's. And I wouldn't even have to wear a veil. My braces were coming off. My orthodontist had said my teeth were ready. I could smile till the cows came home.

"You must be imagining things," I said as R.J. helped me finish folding the sheet. "You'd know for sure if your mom was really planning to move. She'd be selling your apartment and packing and . . ."

"That's what I keep telling myself," he said.

"And you were absolutely right not to mention

this to anybody but me," I told him. "You'd cause a lot of trouble for nothing. So we'll keep this a secret, okay? I swear I won't tell a soul."

And I really meant that.

...11

A long time ago Minna told me it was too bad that nobody wanted to hire a couple of good yentas.

"If anybody did," she said, "and you and I went professional, we could make a fortune."

I agreed. I knew "yenta" was a Yiddish word for a busybody who loves to gossip. And Minna and I do have big mouths. I'll admit it. Being yentas would have been perfect careers for us.

But there are two things I've kept strictly to myself.

Seeing my dad break down and cry the day he and Mom split up was one of them. I've never told anybody. I wasn't quite nine then, and I thought my heart would break watching Dad move his books and clothes out of our house. I couldn't bear to stay and see him drive away in the van he had rented. Without saying goodbye, I tore through the woods to the duck pond and sat there till the sun went down, hugging Joy and crying.

Not even Minna knows.

The other thing I kept to myself was a mistake. I should have told. R.J. wasn't imagining anything down in our basement. His mother really was planning to move to London. Of course nobody knew it at the time. Mom and Seth found out eventually—months later. But if they had known sooner, if I'd been more concerned about R.J. and less concerned about wearing my flower girl dress, I could have spared all of us a lot of agony.

But that's jumping way ahead of my story.

The wedding, "our wedding" as Sarah calls it, went off as scheduled on May twenty-seventh. It wasn't exactly a fairy tale wedding where people get married and live happily ever after. But it was definitely a day to remember.

A week before it took place, everything indicated clear sailing ahead.

The weather was perfect. Better than Hawaii. My braces were off and Mom's book jackets were finished. With her deadlines out of the way, she was concentrating completely on last minute details, like our yard. It looked perfect.

The hedges and bushes were all pruned. The lawn had been mowed. In a week's time, the lilacs and dogwood would be in full bloom.

Each day was like a countdown:

On Saturday, May twentieth, Sarah and I went into the city to have Mister Rudy, on the third floor of F. A. O. Schwarz, give us special prewedding haircuts.

On Sunday, May twenty-first, Grandma Benton flew in from Portland, Oregon, carrying two huge suitcases and presents.

Two days later, on the twenty-third, five more relatives arrived. Mom's sister Janet, Uncle Howard and their three kids, our cousins, Chris, Colin and Heather. They had come all the way from Tucson, Arizona.

We had a terrific reunion. It was much better than our last reunion at Grandma's house in Oregon the summer Mom and Dad separated. Sarah and I had cried at the drop of a hat that summer. Mom was worse. She had been so moody and depressed, she'd made everybody else depressed.

Aunt Janet and Grandma were careful not to remind her of it while they were in Briarcliff. Janet just kept hugging Mom and saying to Uncle Howard, "Isn't it wonderful to see Liz her old happy self again?"

Grandma was even more discreet. Whenever she referred to our miserable trip to Oregon, she called it "that other summer" or "you know when." Of course we all knew what she meant. Just the same as Sarah and I knew she was talking about Dad when she said to Janet, "I understand *you-know-who's* new wife is expecting a baby."

With all the talk, talk, talk and excitement of having nine people under the same roof, I didn't want to go to school. Neither did Sarah, but Mom made us, anyway.

I took advantage of being the only girl in my class who had ever been a flower girl. Was everybody jealous. Each recess I had a following of eight to ten green-eyed girls out in the playground, waiting for an up-to-the-minute report.

On Wednesday, I told them about Seth's first meeting with my mother's family. "Grandma really slipped up," I said. "You know what she called Seth? She called him *Bob.*"

On Thursday, I described the oval blue-and-white tent that the catering service had pitched in our backyard. Nine round tables were going inside for the wedding luncheon.

By Friday, the day before the wedding, some of the news had filtered down to Mrs. Worley, my teacher. After lunch she asked me to help her carry a stack of social studies books to the supply room. I knew that meant she wanted a little heart-to-heart talk with me.

Mrs. Worley's specialty, or "knack" as parents call it, is supposed to be her sensitivity to kids. She uses the supply room as an excuse to be alone with anybody in her class who has a problem.

Only I didn't know *I* had a problem.

"Well, Kitty, I hear you're about to have a major change in your life," she said as she took the books out of my hands.

"You mean my mom's wedding?" I said.

Mrs. Worley smiled. "How are you feeling about it? . . . *Inside,* I mean."

"Oh, same as outside," I said.

"A little frightened?"

I shook my head.

"No?" She put the books on a shelf. "Sometimes these adjustments can be difficult. Accepting a stepparent isn't easy . . ."

"But Seth's a super guy," I said. "I'm crazy about him. So's my sister. You ought to meet him."

Mrs. Worley smiled again, but she gave me the impression I'd disappointed her.

Before we left the supply room, she told me she was always available if I ever needed to talk. "It's good when we can get in touch with our real feelings," she said.

I knew she meant well, but it gave me the same kind of pang I'd felt back in fourth grade when I saw a pile of students' confidential folders on my teacher's desk. Mine was one of the top folders. Next to Kitty Birdsall there was a dash, then somebody had written "BROKEN HOME" in red pencil. It looked as if my name were Kitty Birdsall—BROKEN HOME.

I was glad to get out of school. As soon as the bus dropped us off at the bottom of Hastings Street, Sarah, Minna and I dashed up the hill to see what new developments had taken place in our backyard. Plenty. Not only had the caterers set up the tables and chairs inside the tent for the luncheon, they'd set up fifty more chairs on the lawn for the ceremony.

Those chairs were divided into two sections with a runner of white carpet between them, and they faced our weeping willow tree. That was the prettiest spot in our yard. It overlooked our rhododendron garden.

But it was really the weeping willow tree itself that looked most spectacular. In a burst of creativity, Mom and Aunt Janet had spent the afternoon tying the ends of the lower branches to higher branches to make scallops. At the points of each scallop, they had wired bouquets of daisies and streamers of blue satin ribbons.

Chris, Colin and Heather ran outside when they saw us home from school. The six of us skipped and danced and sang under the tree, pretending we were spinning on a runaway merry-go-round. I almost didn't have to pretend. I felt so happy and excited, it seemed we really were.

That evening we had the wedding rehearsal.

Since Mom's not Jewish and Seth's not Lutheran, they had compromised on having a Unitarian minister marry them. The minister, the organist and Mom's good friend Carol, who was to be the wedding soloist, came to our house at six. Then all of us, even my cousins, drove to a nearby hotel. At the hotel we met Seth and R.J., who had checked in late in the afternoon with Mama, Papa and Seth's friend Herb, who was to be the best man.

There were seventeen of us altogether. We had an early, quick dinner then we headed back to our house for the rehearsal. The caterers hadn't left us much to do. They had already set up the portable electric organ in the back of the tent. Seth simply carried the sixty-foot cord across our yard and plugged it into the socket near our back door.

Then we were ready.

I doubt if any Broadway show ever went smoother than that rehearsal. Everybody said what he or she was supposed to say, did what he or she was supposed to do. And the music was first rate. Carol sang "Greensleeves" so beautifully it gave me goose bumps.

But not one person out of the seventeen people present thought to listen to the latest weather forecast. While we were having a good time, there was a sudden shift in some easterly winds. The probability of rain for the weekend had leaped from ten percent to ninety percent. And none of us knew.

The first thing that crossed my mind when I woke up the next morning was . . . it's here! It's *really* here! The day of the wedding! Then my cousin Colin, who was sharing my room, told me it was raining. I didn't know how that was possible. Briarcliff had looked like the South Pacific all week . . . It was supposed to stay that way: Colin has to be kidding, I thought, until I peeked out the window.

He wasn't. It was. But not hard . . . only a slight drizzle.

"Maybe the sun will be out by noon," Mom said at ten, three hours before the wedding.

I guess the caterers weren't as opimistic. Before they left on Friday, they had covered the chairs on the lawn with plastic sheets and left the white carpet runner rolled up inside the tent.

We found a crew of five men in work overalls ringing our doorbell at ten-thirty, Saturday morning. Mom hadn't expected anyone from the catering service that early. A truck was parked in our driveway and one of the men asked Mom if she wanted to use their alternate plan.

"*What* alternate plan?" she said.

The short, stocky guy who was the spokesman said, "Well, if we could stack the nine luncheon tables somewhere, like in your garage, Mrs. Birdsall, then we could set up chairs for the ceremony inside the tent. You'd stay dry in there, anyway."

"What about the luncheon afterward?" she said.

"We'd have to bring the tables out to the tent again."

"How long would that take?" she asked.

The stocky guy scratched his chin. "Let's see . . . with moving the other stuff out, and moving the tables in and the linens and centerpieces and place settings and so on and so forth . . . oh, about an hour and a half, more or less."

Mom wasn't taking this too well. Fifty guests would have to hang around inside the house, waiting for lunch.

She stood there, not saying a word. And she looked ghastly. She'd just stepped out of the shower, so she had a big, green towel wrapped around her hair like a turban. Worse, she was wearing a robe. Her old seersucker summer one with the hole.

I was praying the caterers didn't know she was the bride.

"Well?" said the spokesman.

When Mom didn't answer, Grandma tried being helpful. She said, "Liz, dear, I have an idea. Why don't you have the ceremony right here in your living room? That way your guests wouldn't have to wait for lunch . . . They could go directly out to the tent and . . ."

Mom didn't even let her finish. "I *can't* get married in the living room, Mother!" she said like a witch. "I haven't cleaned the house. I've been too busy with the yard all month!"

We ended up with the alternate plan.

The tent didn't look too bad once the flowers were in it. Mom had ordered eight, high white wicker stands filled with white lilacs and white tulips. The caterers stood four of them on each side of the white carpet aisle, then they brought out what Mom called her "pièce de résistance"—a lilac-covered arbor she had designed to go under the weeping willow tree. It was placed at the front end of the tent.

At a quarter to one, as all the guests were arriving, the rain stopped.

The sun came out. The grass glistened and the dogwoods sparkled. Our yard was in full technicolor. But it was too late to switch back to the original plan. We had to proceed. Mom, who now looked radiant and beautiful in her pale parchment-colored dress, was acting like a woman in love again. And she had a moment of inspiration.

Why couldn't the sides of the tent be rolled up?

All around, say, so the top of the tent would be like an umbrella?

The caterers said, sure—there wouldn't be any problem. They waited until all the guests were seated, then just as the organist began playing, they began rolling. The sides were going up. From where I was standing by the back door with Sarah, Mom, Aunt Janet and Uncle Howard, it was as thrilling as theater curtain time.

This was it! Mom was about to become Mrs. Seth Krampner.

Sarah and I fluffed out the skirts of our lavender dresses. Aunt Janet readjusted the knot of yellow roses pinned in the back of Mom's hair. Then Uncle Howard handed each of us our bouquets.

Sarah went first. When she was about ten paces across the lawn, I followed behind her. Next was Aunt Janet, then Mom on the arm of Uncle Howard who was giving her away.

We entered through the back of the tent, walking in procession to "The Wedding March":

> *Ta tum tee tum*
> *Ta tum tee tum*
> *Ta tuddeldy tee ta*
> *Tum tee tum tum tee tum . . .*

My heart skipped, listening to it. Everyone was standing. I was supposed to look straight ahead, but I couldn't. My head kept turning as if someone were pulling strings attached to my ears. First I looked to

119

the right. There I saw all the familiar faces from Wesleyan Press—the president, his wife . . . the art director who had introduced Mom and Seth.

Over to the left, I saw our neighbors. A whole row of Millens, the Murphys, and up ahead of them, the Shapiros, with Minna sitting next to her mother. Good old Minna. I knew *I* was the moment she'd been waiting for. Here I was . . . a real flower girl! And no braces on my teeth. I felt so proud I walked straighter than a fence post for her. Then we waved. Hers was a little wave with her fingers. Mine was under my bouquet.

There was a lump in my throat as I passed her.

Then my head rotated back to the right. I saw Seth's sister Bernice, who had flown in from San Francisco. Ahead of her were Seth's older sisters, Enid and Diane, with their families. Andy was by the aisle. He had a grin so big when he saw me coming, his mouth looked like the side of a canoe. It made me grin.

In front of him were Mama and Papa. Mama was dabbing her eyes with a hanky, the same as Grandma Benton was doing over on the other side. With her were my cousins Chris, Colin and Heather.

tum tum tee tum!

I was at the end of the aisle.

Seth was already in front of the flower arbor, waiting for Mom. Standing beside him was Herb, the best man. Next to Herb was R.J., holding the two gold rings. It was going just the way we rehearsed it.

I made a sharp left turn and stepped up to my place beside Sarah. Both of us watched Aunt Janet, Mom and Uncle Howard walk to the end of the aisle and take their places.

We all faced forward, smiling. Then, for the first time, we saw the same unobstructed view of our yard that our guests had seen since the tent flaps were raised. Directly ahead was a small clearing in the wooded corner of our property. In the clearing was our dilapidated tool shed. Parked next to the tool shed were two overflowing garbage cans.

Usually Mom left our garbage cans by the garage.

"Why do you think she moved them out there?" Sarah whispered.

"I guess she was trying to hide them," I said.

"It didn't work."

I nodded.

Then the minister took over.

His talk wasn't preachy; none of that scary business about what happens to people who commit sins, etc. He talked about love and partnership.

"Marriage isn't the fairy tale ending of a courtship," was the way he began, "rather, it is the joyous beginning of a great new adventure . . ."

He went on for another ten minutes, telling us how Mom and Seth's adventure would help create a more loving world. Then I noticed something that made me tune out for a while.

I'd seen Plutzie, Sarah's cat, sneak into the tent.

Not much of her, just a yellow streak zip past my leg. Did she have something in her mouth? I wasn't sure until I heard, "peep . . . peep," then a terrible munching noise going on behind me.

Little Heather, who was only five, started crying.

"Now, now, dear," Grandma Benton whispered to her. "He was a very *naughty* little birdie."

I knew better. Plutzie would go after any bird, good or bad. Darn cat. I hated her.

"Your dumb cat's eating a bird," I whispered to Sarah.

She was too caught up in the ceremony to hear me. Mom and Seth were promising to stick together through sickness and health, through richer and poorer and until "death do us part." I peeked around Sarah to watch them exchange rings.

"Do you, Seth Jacob, take this woman to be your lawful wedded wife?" asked the minister.

"I do," said Seth.

"And do you, Elizabeth Joan, take this man to be your lawful wedded husband?"

"I do," said Mom.

The minister pronounced them husband and wife, and just as he did, I saw Mom smile in a way I'll never forget. It said better than any song or any poem how happy she felt. Seth saw it, too, and leaned over and kissed her.

Watching them gave me a funny little fluttery feeling in my stomach. They were married.

The minister said a few more words, blessing their union, then we had music. The organist played a long

Mendelssohn number by herself, then the introduction to "Greensleeves." I could feel goose bumps coming again as Carol began singing, smooth and mellow; the kind of voice you'd say was golden-orange if you gave voices color.

Along about the line,

"Greensleeves was all my *joy* . . ." a little quarter beagle on the porch heard her name and joined in, howling *"Waaa-oooo, waaa-ooooo . . ."*

"Greensleeves was my delight . . ."

"Waaaa-ooooo . . . waaaaa-ooooo . . ."

"Greensleeves was my heart of gold . . ."

"Waaaaa-ooooooooo, waaaa-oooooo . . ."

"And who-ooo . . ."

"Waaaaa-oooo . . ."

". . . but my Laaa-dy Greensleeves?"

". . . Waaaaa-ooooooooooooo."

Once Joy gets going, there's no quitting. Everybody was laughing. Except me, of course. *Why hadn't I put her in the basement?*

Because I'd forgotten!

The only thing I could do would be to duck out of the tent for a few minutes and drag her down there. Darn dog.

"Waaaaaaa-ooooooooooooo . . ."

I ran across the yard, holding my bouquet, then tugged open the porch door, saying, "Bad Joy!" As soon as she saw me, she stopped howling and lay down on the floor like a bath mat with her paws covering her eyes. It's one of her old tricks. She's done it since she was a pup to make me feel guilty.

"Okay, I'm sorry . . . You're a good doggie," I said. "But you can't sing with the lady. Come on."

She followed me as far as the kitchen, then shot off for the living room to hide under the couch when she realized where I was taking her. Hiding under there is another one of her old tricks. To get her out, I'd have to feed her.

I got a hamburger patty out of the refrigerator, brought it in and set it on the floor about a foot away from the couch. When she came crawling out to snatch it, I grabbed her collar and away we went.

The ceremony was over by the time I got outside again. The guests were all milling around the yard in the sun, talking to each other, and Mom was telling the caterers she had changed her mind about eating lunch inside the tent. She wanted them to set the tables in a circle around the weeping willow tree.

The tables were completely ready, down to the last champagne glass, when we finished greeting the guests in the reception line. Everybody was in good spirits and the line was fun. As the Shapiros went through, Minna and I curtsied to each other, pretending we were royalty.

"Dahling, you rally must drop in at the castle one day," she said.

"Oh, but of course, my dear," I said, trying to imitate Queen Elizabeth. "I'll have my coachman get in touch with your lady-in-waiting *immedjately.*"

Andy was the real surprise.

"How'd you do it?" he whispered when he came up to me.

"Do what?" I said.

"Train your dog to sing like that?"

"Why? Are you interested in training Kami-kaze?"

He nodded.

"It's an awful, awful lot of work," I said.

"I don't care . . . I'm willing," he said. "Listen, if I give you a buck, would you send me a letter with instructions?"

I said sure, then we shook hands on the deal, me smiling and thinking what a dope he was. All I was going to tell him was to howl and howl till he got Kamikaze howling.

He started to walk off, then came back. "Hey, I almost forgot to tell you something," he whispered. "I made a mint on Jump-Over-the-Bridge."

"How? By betting?"

"Uh-uh. I typed the rules, xeroxed them and sold them for a buck apiece."

A camera was clicking.

Cameras were all over the place. Half the guests had come equipped with them, knowing that Seth couldn't take any pictures during the ceremony. He had to wait until we were all seated around the weeping willow tree, eating jellied consommé, cold salmon and puffy little finger rolls before he could start taking his own pictures.

His camera clicked nonstop as he and Mom made the rounds from table to table, thanking everybody, individually, for coming to their wedding. Neither of them sat down until it was time to uncork the champagne bottles and have a toast.

Herb's toast was first. It was full of funny advice

for the bride and groom and had all of us laughing. A few other people made toasts after his, but it was Papa's I remember most.

His was last. He waited till it was quiet, then he stood, adjusting his hearing aid, looked around, and in a shaky voice he said, "When Mama and I came here today, I said to her, 'Mama, isn't this how the Book of Life began . . . with a man and a woman in a beautiful garden?' Mama didn't answer for a moment. She was so quiet, I thought perhaps she hadn't heard. I was about to repeat my question when she said to me, 'Papa, think! Think how lucky we are that *this* book begins on the second chapter . . .'"

As he spoke, he smiled at Sarah and me. Mom and Seth were smiling, too. I knew Papa's toast meant something about us, but I wasn't sure in what way. Then I felt his hand touch my shoulder and he went on . . .

". . . I speak for Mama and myself and every member of our family in saying how blessed we are that the daughter who joins our lives today brings with her the gifts of a separate beginning. To you, Liz, Sarah and Kitty . . . La Chaim!"

There was a murmuring of "La Chaims"—to long life—around the tree as he sat down.

For a moment, I couldn't look up. He had said the nicest thing anyone ever said about us. The "separate beginning" was Mom's marriage to Dad and by the "gifts," he had meant Sarah and me. Were we? I felt sort of embarrassed. What if other people didn't think so? Papa always had a way of making me wish I were a better person.

Maybe I wouldn't charge Andy a dollar for telling him how to train Kamikaze to howl.

Mom and Seth were cutting their cake. I glanced at R.J., who was sitting between me and Sarah, watching them.

"Did you mean it when you said 'La Chaim'?" I whispered.

"You mean after Grandpa's toast?"

"Yes, did you *really* mean it?"

"Of course I did," he said.

Our champagne glasses were filled with 7-Up. I raised mine and tapped the rim of his. "La Chaim to you, too," I said, smiling as I added, "Stepbrother."

He smiled back.

Like it or not, for better or for worse, from this day forward we were a family.

...12

The number of people staying in our house dwindled down to three the day after the wedding. Sarah, me and Grandma Benton. Everybody else left. Aunt Janet and her family went back to Arizona and Mom and Seth flew up to Quebec for a five-day honeymoon.

Grandma took a little getting used to once she was in charge. She was a real worrywart. But she was still fun.

Before Sarah and I left for school each morning, she fixed us pancakes with smiley faces made out of blueberries or banana slices. In the afternoons when we came home, she showed us how to crochet, or she baked sourdough bread and told us stories about Mom and Aunt Janet when they were little.

We were sorry to see her go back to Oregon. She left the day after Mom and Seth came home from

Canada. Then we had to get down to serious packing so we could move.

What a job! Sarah, Mom and I are class-A collectors. *Were,* rather. Seth changed us. When he saw all the old toys and junk we had accumulated in our attic and basement, he told Mom if she was planning to take it to Soho, we'd have to call in the Marines.

Mom decided to have a tag sale.

The idea was to get rid of surplus: things we'd never need again like baby furniture, garden tools, our lawnmower, snowblower, etc. etc. It came to over three hundred miscellaneous items. We tagged them all and put ads in the local papers.

The day of the sale, three or four times as many people showed up as we'd had at the wedding. Items such as outgrown skates and our wheelbarrow moved fast. Mom got so carried away taking bids and selling that when a woman made her an offer on the dining room set, she sold it. Next went the chandelier.

After that, Mom opened the doors to the living room, kitchen and den. Anything that wasn't plugged in or nailed down, disappeared before our eyes.

By the time the sale was over, half our furniture was gone. "I guess we won't need the Marines, after all," Seth said. "We can mail what's left to the city in an envelope."

I didn't laugh. Our couches were sold and I wanted to know what we were going to sit on in the loft. Mom told me not to worry, she'd thought of a solution. The carpenters would build us something called a "conversation pit."

I was glad she hadn't let anybody upstairs to buy our beds.

We moved one week to the day after school was out. Sarah and I didn't sleep at our house that last night. She stayed with her best friend Jamie, and I stayed with Sally Doolittle. No, I'm kidding. Anybody who knows me, knows I wouldn't have spent my last night in Briarcliff with anybody other than my very dearest, closest, most loyal friend in the whole world, Minna Shapiro.

We cried all night.

Then we cried again the next morning when the Mayflower moving van pulled out of our driveway at 311 Hastings Street. And I cried even harder when I called her from the city that afternoon to tell her how much I hated the loft.

"There's plumbing in only one bathroom," I said, "and that bathroom doesn't even have walls."

I wasn't exaggerating. All it had on the sides were wooden two-by-fours mounted every eighteen inches.

The plasterboard walls were nailed to the two-by-fours the next day while we were having our first visit from our new neighbors, the Lebowitzes. They welcomed us to Soho with a platter of vegetable tempura. And the reason I remember that they brought it over the same day the bathroom walls went up was because I happened to be taking a bath when the buzzer rang.

Sarah opened the door before I had a chance to

grab a towel and run to my room. I just had to sit in the tub, watching all nine Lebowitzes file in.

Mrs. Lebowitz was at the head of the procession, carrying the tempura. Behind her were six boys. Behind the boys were Mr. Lebowitz and the baby, also a boy. Behind them were the carpenters carrying the plasterboards.

Except for the bathtub incident and saying goodbye to R.J. when when he left for camp in July, my memories of the summer are mostly of living out of a suitcase and trying to adjust to confusion. Renovating is no picnic. It means dust, noise, holes in your floors, wires, pipes and lots of cranky workmen. The best remedy was to get away from the loft.

As Seth had promised before we moved, we got acquainted with the neighborhood restaurants. We didn't have much choice. Either we ate out, or we stayed home in the mess and heated TV dinners in our toaster oven. So we ate out.

Some nights we walked over to Mott and Mulberry Streets in Chinatown. Other nights we went down to the Lower East Side to get blintzes smothered in sour cream at one of the kosher dairy restaurants.

Wherever we went, Seth took his camera. He was doing an article on New York's ethnic restaurants for a travel magazine.

In the daytime, while he developed pictures, Mom worked at her drawing board and the carpenters hammered, Sarah and I went exploring. Coming out of our building on Greene Street, we could look south and see the tops of the World Trade Center, two of the tallest buildings in the world. A block away, on the corner of Prince Street, we found a narrow five-story building that had twenty-five windows on the side. Twenty-three of them were fakes. They'd been painted over the brick on the outside. The two real ones had air conditioners.

At first Sarah and I didn't stray very far. Either we took Joy for a short walk, or we went to the playground. With the encouragement of Max and Mordecai Lebowitz, the oldest of the seven Lebowitz boys, we got more adventurous. Max was eleven and Mordecai was thirteen and they knew Soho and the surrounding neighborhoods the way Marco Polo must have known China.

On our first outing with them, they asked if we wanted to visit places that grownups didn't like very much, but that kids did. We said sure, so they took us to the side streets of the Bowery. I was a little scared. Everywhere we looked, we saw guys with stained shirts and worn-out shoes with no socks, who were sprawled out on the sidewalks or in doorways drinking out of bottles in brown paper bags.

Mordecai said they were all harmless. He knew quite a few of them by name. He'd say, "There's old Bill Brummett . . . That's his doorway." Then he'd wave and if the guy lying in the doorway wasn't snoring like a buzz saw, he'd look up at Mordecai and say, "Howyadoin, kid?"

Max told us these were no ordinary bums. They

were famous. "You ask anybody who comes to New York if they know what the Bowery's famous for," he said, "and they'll tell you, 'you bet . . . the Bowery bums.' "

On the way home, we got lemon ices from a street vendor and walked through Chinatown to see the plucked chickens and ducks hanging in the butcher shop windows. They still had heads and feet and were extremely gross, but I knew Minna would want to see them when she came to the city.

She rode the train in for her first visit with us a few days later. After Sarah and I showed her the loft, we took her out for an afternoon of sightseeing. We said the choice was up to her—we could go to the Central Park Zoo, the Empire State Building or to the Bowery and Chinatown.

Of course we knew what she'd choose.

We spent most of our time in Chinatown. We looked at the ducks and chickens, then we wandered in and out of variety stores, trying to help Minna find a souvenir. She couldn't decide between chopsticks and a wicker cricket box. Finally she bought incense.

Our last stop was the Bowery. As we passed the doorway of a ramshackle tenement on Broome Street, I nudged Minna. "That's Bill Brummett," I said.

He heard me and looked up from his brown paper bag.

I knew Minna was impressed that I'd learned so much about the city in such a short time.

R.J. had a different reaction. The day before he

left for camp, Sarah and I gave him the same tour we'd given Minna. Only we started with the Bowery. He'd never been there and he was really shocked.

"Such terrible suffering," he said when he saw Bill Brummett stretched out in his doorway.

"Then why's he snoring?" asked Sarah.

R.J. didn't answer. He reached in his pocket for change and stuck it under Bill's brown bag. "I'm writing to the mayor tonight . . . before I leave for camp," he said, "and I'm going to demand better rehabilitation facilities."

"What're those?" Sarah said.

"Places where these unfortunate men can get well."

She and I decided to bypass the Chinese butcher shops. We didn't think R.J. was in the mood for them. We bought ices, then walked back to Soho along another street, stopping to show him a telephone booth designed like a pagoda. It was amazing, we thought, that a rich kid who had lived in New York all his life had never been to any good places.

On the corner of Prince and Greene, we pointed out the building with the fake windows. R.J. liked that, and he liked the African art gallery across from our building. What interested him the most, though, was a strange, slinky, four-legged animal that a woman was leading on a leash to the shop next to the art gallery.

I was more fascinated by the woman. She had frizzy pink hair.

R.J. went over to her before she opened the shop door. "Excuse me, is your pet a ferret?" he asked.

"Why yes, she is," said the woman. "Do you have one?"

He shook his head. "No, but I've read about ferrets. I understand they're related to polecats."

Sarah and I crouched down to the sidewalk to get a better look. I would have guessed the animal was a weasel.

"Isn't she a sweetie?" said the woman. "Her name's Lila and you can all pet her if you want."

Sarah and I waited for R.J. to go first. We hadn't forgotten Fred, the bloodthirsty gerbil Minna had in third grade. I have a scar on my finger, thanks to Fred.

R.J. didn't seem a bit afraid of Lila. He held out his hand so she could sniff it, then he scratched behind her ears and stroked her long, furry neck. "She's very gentle," he said.

The pink-haired lady smiled. "She's expecting little kits in a few weeks. Would you like to come see them when they're born?"

"Oh, yes. Very much," said R.J. "But I'm leaving for camp in Vermont tomorrow . . . I won't be back till the end of August."

"Leave me your name and phone number, anyway," she said. "I'll call your mother, then you can come by and see them when you get home."

R.J. eyed me, looking panicked. "Kitty, do you mind if I give her your number instead?"

"No, go ahead," I said.

The woman dug through her fringed purple shoulder bag for a pad and pencil. The outfit she had on was the wildest I'd ever seen—red textured tights, silver boots, a top made out of crocheted pot holders, green shorts and a snake bracelet. It almost made you forget her pink hair.

She was nice, though. And very friendly. She told us her name was Lottie . . . Lottie Pinkham, and she lived in the back of her shop. "This is it right here," she said, pointing to the sign over the window: CLOTHES ENCOUNTERS.

R.J. noticed she had her pencil ready.

He gave her our names, I gave her our phone number and Sarah told her where our loft was, how long we'd lived there, what the carpenters were doing, our life's history and how the three of us were related.

Lottie seemed interested in every tidbit. "So your father's their stepfather?" she said to R.J. He nodded. "Well, I'm a real sucker for kids," she went on, "so you all drop in to see me any time you want . . . okay? You can try on the vests I make."

Crossing the street to go home, R.J. apologized for asking me to use our number instead of his. It was because of his mother. "I'd have a hard time explaining why Lottie was calling her about ferrets," he said.

The very thought seemed to make him sweat.

That was the last time we saw him until the end of August. He said goodbye to us after dinner and promised he'd write. We said we would, too. Then Seth took him home.

Sarah and I were waiting up for Seth when he came back. We knew he was bringing Shirley home because weeks earlier we'd told R.J. we'd take care of her.

And I have to admit I thought Shirley was cute. According to the weight chart attached to her cage, she weighed twenty-nine ounces. Most of her is shaggy hair. In my first letter to R.J., I wrote that I was having a hard time telling which end of her was which.

We got a lot of letters from him at Camp Wamapausett. His private ones to me were so long and detailed I could picture the kids in his bunk and taste the lumpy mashed potatoes they ate for dinner.

I started making my letters more detailed. If the carpenters pounded in a new nail, I told him.

As the summer wore on, he and I began writing each other our deepest secrets. He told me he had a complex about his pointed nose and being uncoordinated. I wrote back and said I'd only noticed his nose.

In my next letter, I made a confession: I told him about the night Minna and I tricked Sarah into spilling the beans about his birthday checks from his Grandfather Lerner. "Don't blame Sarah," I said in the P.S. "She doesn't remember anything."

I gave that letter to Mom and Seth to deliver to R.J. in person when they drove to Vermont for Parents' Visiting Day, the end of July.

They were gone three days and while they were away, Sarah and I stayed with Dad and Linda. We had been taking the train to Croton almost every weekend all summer. Linda was getting as big as a two-family house. The bigger she grew, the more excited we became about the baby. Sometimes when it kicked, she put our hands on her stomach so we could feel. To me it was a miracle.

"What are you naming this little kickeroo?" I asked.

"Andrea if it's a girl . . . Joshua if it's a boy," she said.

I was relieved that she and Dad weren't considering Charlotte or Wilbur.

Croton was a nice contrast to Soho. After listening to banging and hammering all week, Sarah and I could hardly wait to get up there. Meals were on schedule, the house was neat and clean and Dad always had soft classical music playing on the stereo. But one of the best bonuses, as far as I was concerned, was being close enough to see Minna.

Sometimes Dad dropped me off in Briarcliff for an afternoon. Sometimes Minna's parents brought her to Croton. The Shapiros hadn't taken sides when Mom and Dad got divorced. Dad was still Minna's pediatrician and Mrs. Shapiro and Linda had become good friends.

By Sunday night, Sarah and I were usually anxious to get back to Soho. Maybe we're crazy, but after a weekend of peace and quiet, we missed noise.

Riding into the city together, we always agreed that we were lucky to have two homes.

...13

Sometime around the beginning of August, Lottie called to invite Sarah and me to see Lila's kits. "Lila had three of them," she said, "and they're just opening their eyes."

We asked Max and Mordecai Lebowitz if they wanted to go down to her shop with us. We knew they would, because they like animals. Max has a ribbon snake and several hermit crabs and Mordecai has a tortoise a little bigger than a crash helmet. "Toots" he calls her.

The shop had a distinct odor. If I had to compare it with anything, I'd say it was close to sweaty gym socks with a bit of skunk smell mixed in. We just followed our noses to the box behind the counter. Lila was inside, watching us suspiciously as we bent down to see her three nuzzling fuzz balls.

"She might be a bit nippy if you try to touch

them," said Lottie. So we didn't. We just had a nice chat with Lottie who comes from Arkansas. She'd moved to New York to be a jazz singer, she said, but here she was, making vests out of soda can flip tops instead.

We loved the vests. The four of us tried them on after we had the cold drinks Lottie brought us from her back room. It was terrific the way she linked the vests together. You could hardly tell they were flip tops.

I was dying, absolutely dying, to have one for school.

When we got home, I described them to Mom, and told her they cost thirty dollars. "If you get me one, I won't ask for another thing all year," I said. "Not even underwear."

She said she'd have to think about it, which surprised me. If I'd asked her for a flip-top vest while we were living in Briarcliff, she would have given me a flat "no."

Her hopeful answer meant one thing: we were getting used to the artsy-craftsy styles of Soho. Even Mom. She was wearing gauzy skirts and blouses, hoop earrings and doing her hair differently. Almost every day now, she put it in a single braid that hung down between her shoulder blades. Seth liked it. "The real me is emerging," Mom told him the first time she wore it.

I wrote R.J. about the vests and Lila's kits. While I was waiting for him to answer, I realized how much

I missed him. Maybe not in the same sort of nagging, toothache way I missed Minna, but I sure thought about him. I was crossing off the days on the calendar till he came home.

His twelfth birthday was August sixteenth. I spent hours pasting dried peas and beans on a piece of cardboard. They spelled "Happy XII" in Roman numerals. I clipped a note on the back, telling him I was saving his present for when he got home.

The truth was, I was still making it. I'd been working on a photo album of animal pictures throughout the summer. The pictures were taken by me with my own camera and each time I finished a roll of film, Seth and I went into the makeshift darkroom he'd set up next to our unfinished kitchen.

In there he taught me all the steps of processing. First we wrapped the film around a reel. Next we put the reel into a canister and poured smelly chemical gunk over it. Then we hung the wet film up to dry, weighting it with clothespins so it wouldn't curl. And finally, we put it in the photo enlarger and mounted it on frames.

The album was completely finished the day R.J. arrived home from camp. We had a dual belated-birthday and homecoming celebration for him that night. Mama and Papa drove in from Queens and Sarah and I stuck a sign on the front door that said:

> *Roses are red*
> *Coal is black*
> *We're tickled pink*
> *To have R.J. back.*

Rather than going out for dinner, we ordered Chinese food from Sun Wo Ping and ate it on Mom's drawing board laid flat across two sawhorses. Dessert was ice cream with Mama's homemade chocolate buttermilk cake. I zipped through the meal, chewing fast, because I couldn't wait for R.J. to open his presents.

Mine was at the bottom of the pile. I'd purposely put it there because I wanted it saved for last.

R.J. didn't rip off the wrapping paper the way I do. He removed it carefully, undoing the tape. But I knew he liked the album. He turned the pages, one by one, looking at each and every picture. As he finished each page, he held it up so everybody else could see.

Mama adored the picture of a dog sharing a pretzel with a little girl in a stroller.

"Where'd you take it, darling?" she asked me.

"In the playground," I said.

"Well, it could win a prize . . . a *first* place prize, couldn't it, Papa?"

Papa said he thought every picture in the album could win a first prize.

I have to admit I was proud. There were pictures of Shirley sleeping, Plutzie watching her, Joy sniffing an electrician . . . tons of pictures of the Lebowitzes' pets, Lila and her kits and every animal I'd seen while I was exploring Soho.

R.J. didn't say he had a favorite, but I noticed he spent the most time looking at the picture on the last page. It was a blowup of Mordecai's tortoise, Toots, walking across the wet tile in the Lebowitzes' kitchen.

Later, when he and Sarah and I were alone, R.J. told us he'd enjoyed camp more than he expected. "Most of the kids weren't any more athletic than I am," he said. "Neither were the counselors . . . Camp Klutz, we called it. I made a couple of good friends."

I didn't have a whole lot of questions to ask him about camp because he'd told me what I wanted to know in his letters.

But Sarah had a question: Did he or any of his friends ever go skinny-dipping? R.J. told her no. Then she got around to the one question she'd been itching to ask all evening: Had he received his birthday check from his Grandfather Lerner?

R.J. said he had. His mother had forwarded it to him the week before.

"Well-l? What're you buying with it?"

"Nothing," he said. "I've decided to do something else with it."

"Put it in your trust fund?"

R.J. told her no, but of course Sarah wouldn't let up. She said, "Well, what *are* you going to do with it?"

He asked her if she remembered the day the three of us walked through the Bowery. Sarah said she did; she remembered. Then R.J. asked her if she remembered what he'd said that day about writing to the mayor. Again Sarah said she did.

"Well, I wrote . . . I wrote to him that night," he said, "and a week later I got a letter from him at camp saying . . ."

"Hey, hold it!" said Sarah. "You mean *the* mayor

of New York City? . . . He wrote to *you?* Wow! What did the kids at camp think? That you knew him?"

"I didn't tell any of them," said R.J.

"Didn't tell any of them?"

At this point I had to tell Sarah to shut up. R.J. hadn't told *me* about the letter, either. "So what did the mayor say?" I asked.

"Oh, he was very nice. He explained that the city is always working on programs to help those indigent men we'd seen. But he said there's never enough money. So I've decided to donate my check to the Bowery Home for the Homeless."

I thought about that for days and days afterward. R.J. didn't just dream about making the world a better place the way most of us do. He really tried.

...14

No ducks ever took to water faster than Sarah and I took to Soho Community School in September. We liked it from Day One, which is good—we'll be there a while. SCS goes all the way through the ninth grade.

What makes it different from other schools is that the students are encouraged to do their own thing. If you want to be a composer, that's fine. If you've got your heart set on becoming a shepherd, that's fine, too.

Most of the kids like to paint. The walls on all four floors are covered with artwork. You might see something as far-out as Mordecai's painting of an idea passing through his brain cells, but you'll never see twenty-five identical styrofoam snowmen hanging in the halls.

The teachers let us call them by their first names if we want and they're dedicated to creativity.

That's why Mom chose the school. It's also why Dad was against it. But only initially. He started coming round after Sarah and I had been enrolled there for three weeks.

The following weekend, she and I stayed in Croton.

Driving to the house from the train station, Dad said, "Tell me something, Sarah . . . What's so special about SCS?"

"We don't get pages of busywork," she said.

Dad thought a minute, then he looked at me. "What do you think is so special, Kitty?"

"Attitudes."

"Such as?"

"Such as not having any kids there from broken homes," I said.

"What about you and Sarah?"

"*We* come from extended families," I said.

Dad smiled as he turned the car into the driveway.

He and Sarah and I didn't know it then, but our family was going to get even more extended before the weekend was over.

Our first signal came at eight-thirty the next morning. That's breakfast time in Croton and Linda didn't have scrambled eggs and toast on the table. We knew something was up. Her schedules never vary.

At nine-thirty, Dad called Linda's ex-husband in

Tarrytown to tell him to plan on keeping Peter and Sylvia a few extra days. Linda was in labor.

At ten we drove her to the hospital. At noon, Sarah and I were looking through the nursery window at Joshua Alan Birdsall. That's right . . . our little brother Josh!—the reddest, baldest, most god-awful wrinkly looking kid anybody ever laid eyes on.

"Are you *positive* he isn't the cute baby with hair?" Sarah asked one of the nurses.

"No, that's the Mortarotti baby," the nurse said.

Sarah and I pressed our noses flat against the nursery window and kept looking. Within five minutes we were madly in love with that little red, bald guy in the bassinet. Neither of us could stop grinning.

"Isn't ugly wonderful?" Sarah said.

Josh was barely two weeks old when I knew I had to do my share to help make the world a better place.

What brought about my decision was a discussion my social studies class had one afternoon early in October about the famine in Zaire, Africa.

Like the teacher and most of the kids in my class, I'd read the article about the famine in the *New York Times.* Hundreds of thousands of people were starving. It broke my heart to look at the pictures of babies with protruding ribs and swollen stomachs.

I thought about Josh. He was so lucky. He'd left the hospital just twelve days before to go home to a room decorated with bunny wallpaper and mobiles.

The little babies in Zaire didn't even have milk.

Sitting in class, I knew I had to help. I didn't have much money. Over the summer I'd saved part of my allowance to buy Josh a stuffed animal when he was born. But he already had two teddy bears in his crib. I wondered if he would mind if I sent the seven dollars I'd saved to Zaire instead.

When Sarah and I got home from school, Mom and Seth took a break from their work and we walked over to Houston Street to get ice-cream cones. Going there, I talked about the people in Zaire. I told Mom and Seth I was thinking of sending them the money I'd saved over the summer to help feed the hungry babies.

They had read the *New York Times* article and they liked the idea.

Coming home, we passed Lottie's shop. I steered everybody right up to the vests in the window, reminding them that I had a birthday coming up on October sixteenth.

Mom laughed. "I guess this is a hint."

Hinting is exactly what I was doing. I'd been dying for a vest for two months. And I'm sure I would have said I was if I hadn't seen my reflection in the window.

Just as I did, a little Jiminy Cricket in my head shouted, *"Shame on you, Kitty! You can give up Josh's present for Zaire. But you can't give up your own present, can you?"*

I turned away from the window and Seth put his arm around me. "Kitty, if you'd really like a vest for your birthday, we'll get you one."

"What about those hungry babies?" said my Jiminy Cricket.

I took one last peek at the vests, then turned away again. I told Seth if he and Mom gave me the thirty dollars the vest would cost, I'd have thirty-seven dollars to send to Zaire.

"How would you send it?" Mom asked. "Through the Save the Children Foundation?"

I said I thought so. I'd seen their ads and I knew they helped countries that needed it most.

Seth's arm tightened around my shoulders. "Kitty, if you're really serious about this, your mother and I will match the money you send, dollar for dollar."

I did some quick arithmetic. "You bet I'm serious!"

"Then Zaire just got itself seventy-four dollars," he said.

A few days later, I made a similar arrangement with Dad.

He called to see how Sarah and I were and to find out what train we were taking to Croton over the weekend. When he spoke to me alone, he said he and Linda had been wondering what to get me for my twelfth birthday."

"Would you like a tape recorder?" he asked.

I told him I'd rather send money to help feed the starving children in Zaire.

"You must have read that article in the *New York Times,* too," he said.

I told him I had and put in a plug for SCS: "We talked about it in social studies."

Since he's a pediatrician, it's obvious how he felt about the famine. He said he hadn't stopped thinking about those children all week.

"If it's all right with you," I said, "I'd like to send the money a tape recorder would cost to the Save the Children Foundation."

He didn't answer for a minute. Then he said something that really amazed me. He said, "Honey, if you're willing to do that, then Linda and I are willing to give up the money we've saved so far for a trip to Bermuda this winter."

On October sixteenth, I celebrated my twelfth birthday by sending two checks totalling $774.00 to the Save the Children Foundation.

When Sarah's tenth birthday rolled around on November twelfth, we had gone through nearly a month of upheavals on Greene Street.

First the electricians went on strike.

Then the plumbers.

It seems there are always strikes going on in New York City. For a while we wondered if our loft would ever get finished.

To cut down on the expense of eating out at night, we were depending more and more on our hot plate and toaster oven. I was getting tired of fettucine all'Alfredo. Sarah was getting tired of helping me wash dishes in the bathtub. And we were all getting tired of wallowing through rubble.

Whenever the phone rang, we all scattered in different directions, running and hopping over and around a maze of two-by-fours, sawhorses, wires, pipes and tools. Sometimes we found a phone. Sometimes we didn't.

Mom was sitting at her drawing board just three feet away from a phone the day the school nurse called. That call she got.

"I don't want to alarm you, Mrs. Krampner," the nurse said, "but I think you should take Kitty and Sarah to a dermatologist. They have very suspicious-looking scalp conditions. Possibly nits."

We went to a dermatologist. For fifty dollars he told Mom that Sarah and I had a lot of caked saw-dust. His advice was to start us on a daily ritual of scouring our hairbrushes.

Mom was a little cranky when we left his office. Lately everything had been getting on her nerves. The dust. The noise. Sitting on packing crates. I think she was sorry she'd sold our furniture at the tag sale in June.

Waiting for the freight elevator in our lobby, she complained that we were probably never going to get the modern elevator the real estate agent had prom-ised.

When we got upstairs, she grumped about the dirty clothes in the hampers. Seth and Sarah and I helped her load it into our laundry cart. Then we took Joy and we all went to the laundromat on Prince Street.

By the time we left the laundromat with a week's supply of neatly folded clean clothes, Mom was in a better mood. Even the long wait in the lobby for the elevator didn't seem to bother her once we got back to our building.

"It's taking forever," said a delivery boy who was standing there with a box of groceries for the people in 4-A.

Mom smiled. "Oh, it'll be here."

While we were waiting, Max and Mordecai came in the front door with their mother and four of their little brothers. Not long after they came, we were joined by the poet who lived in the penthouse and his Great Dane.

Eventually the elevator clanked to the lobby.

"Here she is," said the delivery boy.

We all got in. The doors closed. The elevator started up. Just as we were traveling between the third and fourth floors, New York City had one of its famous blackouts. All the electrical power from Fourteenth Street down to Wall Street was cut off. The elevator came to an abrupt stop and the lights went out.

From 4:48 P.M. till 11:56 P.M., thirteen of us and two dogs were stuck in a pitch-black shaft without a bathroom or water.

Dinner was mung bean sprouts and celery from the delivery boy's box of groceries.

The next morning Mom had a mini-breakdown. She locked herself in the bathroom and stayed there for hours, crying. Seth tried talking her into coming out and telling us what was wrong, but she wouldn't.

In desperation, he stuck a chair under the outside doorknob. "Liz, I want to remind you that there are *three* people out in this hall who love you," he hollered. "And if you don't care enough to let us know why you're crying, you can *stay* locked in there!"

That worked. Mom slipped a note under the door which she'd written in lipstick on a long sheet of toilet paper. It was a list of everything bothering her. At the bottom, she said she had found a lump in her breast while she was showering.

I've never been more worried than I was the day she had her operation. Mama and Papa came in from Queens to stay with Sarah and Seth and me in the hospital waiting room. It was terrible waiting. We knew there was a chance Mom could have cancer.

I kept crying and thinking of all the mean things I'd ever said to her. There had been plenty. Once I'd called her a dumb jerk for sending me off to school with a bag of onions instead of my lunch. And I knew she hadn't purposely mixed up the bags.

Now I was sorry.

I cried telling Mama the story. "Another time I told her she was a witch," I said. "But I was just mad at her, Mama . . . Honest I was. I love Mom with all my heart."

Mama wrapped her soft, pillow arms around me. "She knows you do, darling. She knows," she said. Then she let me bury my face in her new pink blouse, not caring that my nose was all runny.

An hour or so later, the surgeon came into the

waiting room with the biopsy report from the lab. Now it was Mama who cried. The tumor was benign; Mom was going to be all right.

Papa kept repeating, "Thank you, doctor . . . thank you," and I heard Seth let out a lungful of air.

"Thank God," he whispered.

Sarah beat me to the punch and asked him if she could be the first person to tell Dad and R.J. the good news. Seth nodded and dug into his pocket to find change for the pay phone.

While Sarah went out to make her calls, I stayed with Mama and Papa, and Seth hurried down to the florist on the main floor of the hospital. He came back carrying so many long-stemmed red roses that they fanned out over the vase like a peacock's tail. He could barely see around them. At the doorway he almost collided with a nurse who was coming in to tell us that Mom was out of the recovery room.

"Aren't those roses *gorgeous!*" she said. Then she peeked in to tell us it would only be a few minutes until we could see Mom. "Of course the hospital has a rule that nobody under the age of fifteen is admitted in a patient's room," she added, looking at me.

My heart sank until I saw her wink. "What are you, dear? About seventeen?"

"About," I said, catching her meaning.

She turned around to leave and this time nearly collided with Sarah. "And how old are you, dear? Twenty-nine or thirty?"

"I am *not!*" said Sarah. "I'm only . . ."

"Now, now." The nurse put her finger up to Sarah's lips. "There's a very nice lady in Room 617 waiting to see her girls," she said. "We wouldn't want to disappoint her by being underage, would we?"

Mom seemed a little groggy from anesthesia when we tiptoed into her room. But her eyes were open and she was smiling. I didn't know if she was in pain, so I hesitated about rushing up to her.

"Does anything hurt?" I whispered from the foot of the bed.

"Only my corn," she mumbled. Then she raised her head off the pillow. "Well, come on! Isn't anybody going to give me a kiss? I'm not nearly as think as you out of it I am!"

That made us laugh for the first time in days. She'd scrambled the words on purpose.

The hospital released her to go home the next morning, but Sarah and Seth and I had planned a surprise. We'd left Joy and Plutzie with the Lebowitzes and packed some suitcases. After we picked Mom up, we drove straight to the Sheraton Hotel and checked in for four days.

Sarah and I missed school for two of them, but neither of us cared. It was great to have a break from the renovations. And we were both so happy and thankful to have Mom well and out of the hospital, we didn't want to leave her side for a minute.

About six times an hour, I told her I loved her.

...15

Sarah gave up a pair of disco roller skates and a clock radio on her tenth birthday. She said she wanted to give money to the American Cancer Society.

No one in our family needed her to explain why.

The night of her birthday, we had a little party for her at the loft. Mama and Papa drove in from Queens and picked up R.J. on their way to Soho.

They brought presents for Sarah, but it wasn't a happy party.

That afternoon, while Sarah and I were in school, Seth received a call from the secretary of R.J.'s school. The secretary told him she had been trying to reach Mrs. Krampner for days, meaning, of course, the *ex*-Mrs. Krampner.

"I thought perhaps you could answer an important question for me," she said.

Seth told her he would try.

"As you know," she went on, "we sent copies of R.J.'s school records to the Lathrop Boys Academy in London nearly two months ago. Now we would like to know . . ."

Seth stopped her right there. He told her he knew absolutely nothing about R.J.'s school records going to London.

"Oh?" The secretary was surprised. She said she was aware that Mrs. Krampner hadn't told R.J. about having his records sent because at the time she made the request, her plans to move to London were indefinite. "But I thought surely she would have informed you," she said.

Seth didn't let on that she had tossed him a bomb. He wanted to get as much information as possible.

"Did Mrs. Krampner tell you *when* she was considering moving?" he asked.

"As I understand it, she was either going to move during the Christmas vacation or at the end of the semester in January."

That was all Seth needed. Now he knew what the secretary's original question was: When was Mrs. Krampner planning to withdraw R.J. from school?

When Sarah and I came home, he was on the phone in our future kitchen, talking to his lawyer. He was boiling mad. Even the carpenters working on the conversation pit in the living room knew. Every time he raised his voice, they stopped sawing.

Sarah and I fixed ourselves snacks and ate them close to the phone so we wouldn't miss a syllable.

157

"You bet I'm ready for another custody battle," he told his lawyer.

Mom, the carpenters and Sarah and I watched him hang up. Before he'd given the phone a chance to cool off, he picked it up again and began dialing.

"Now who're you calling?" Sarah asked through a mouthful of pretzel. "Kay?"

Seth nodded.

"You'd better wait," she said. "If Kay gets mad at you she might not let Mama and Papa bring R.J. to my party."

Seth slammed down the phone. "You're right," he said.

He didn't pussyfoot around when Mama and Papa and R.J. came. He gave them time to take off their coats, sit down and give Sarah her presents, then he said he had something to tell them . . . "Something I'd rather not put off till after dinner," he said.

"Oh, oh. I know by his face he has bad news," Mama whispered up to the ceiling.

Papa clasped his hands and R.J. watched Seth pace the floor with his hands in his pockets. "It's about me, isn't it, Dad?"

Seth took his hands out of his pockets and looked at R.J. "Yes, I'm afraid it is. But before we get into it, I want to ask you something . . . Has your mother ever mentioned taking you to England?"

"Just once," said R.J. "Last week she told me we

might fly to London during the Christmas holidays. I was going to tell you tonight."

"But has she ever mentioned *moving* to London?"

R.J. shook his head. "Uh-uh . . . Never. Why? Do you think she is?"

"She's certainly been making arrangements to move."

Mama gasped. "Kay told you?"

"No, of course not . . . She knew I'd get a court order to stop her. Moving R.J. more than a hundred miles from New York is a violation of our divorce contract!" Seth said. "Kay couldn't even tell *R.J.* for fear he'd tell me, so she's been planning this behind our backs. She knew that once she got him out of the country, my hands were tied."

"How do you know this?" asked Papa.

"I got a call from R.J.'s school secretary this afternoon . . . She let the cat out of the bag." Seth sat down facing everybody, then he spilled out his entire conversation with the secretary.

R.J. turned the color of a mushroom when he heard about the Lathrop Boys Academy. He looked at me and I knew we were thinking the same thing— that we should have told about the registered letter he saw on Kay's desk, months ago.

It was my fault. I'd made him promise not to tell anybody.

He started crying and Sarah went and put her arms around him. "Don't you cry, R.J." she said. "We won't let your mother kidnap you! We're going to have a great big . . ." She stopped and looked at

Seth. "Well-l? Do you want to tell him about the battle or should I?"

Seth couldn't help smiling. "You can, Sarah. But first let me ask him a question."

"Hurry," she said.

"Son, would you like to live here with us?"

R.J. wiped his cheeks with the back of his hand. "You know I do . . . I've always wanted to."

"Oh, good," said Sarah, "because we're gonna have this great big battle with your mother to get custody of you and your dad's already talked to his lawyer and . . ." She took such a deep breath I expected her to puff up. "Okay, Seth . . . *Now* you can call Kay."

Seth spoke to Kay on a phone thirty feet away from us but we still heard what he said to her. They had a terrible argument. We knew what she was saying by listening to what he was saying.

"Oh, come on, Kay . . . Don't deny it and don't tell me I'm paranoid," he said. "I found out through a very reliable source."

I nudged Mom and asked her why Seth didn't tell Kay that his source was the school secretary.

"Because his lawyer told him not to," she whispered.

Seth and Kay must have argued another twenty minutes. It got pretty sticky.

The last thing he said to her was, "Okay, princess, this time you've cooked your goose!"

...16

Kay's goose didn't get cooked soon enough to suit us. R.J. still had to go on living with her, the poor kid. And she made his life miserable. He was such a nervous wreck by the end of November that Seth made sure he started seeing Dr. Mendelmann again.

As for Sarah and me, we certainly expanded our vocabularies listening to all the custody talk. The word that came up most was "hearing," which means a trial that takes place before a judge without a jury.

We had one scheduled for December eleventh. At our hearing, the judge was going to make two decisions: 1) whether Kay should be allowed to take R.J. to London during the Christmas holidays, and 2) whether she should continue having custody of him.

Seth was more worried about the first decision. He knew Kay would lie. She already had. She'd denied ever having any intention of moving to London.

Seth was afraid that if she convinced the judge she was taking R.J. to England for a vacation, and nothing else, he would let her go, she would stay and she'd never bring R.J. back.

So far, Kay had been very clever. She hadn't sold her co-op apartment, shipped her furniture or done any of the obvious things people do when they're planning to move. But then, she didn't need to. As Seth told his lawyer on the phone, Kay had enough money to buy and furnish a house in London without selling her place in New York.

"I think we'd win if we could prove that's what she's done," he said.

His lawyer agreed. He told Seth he was doing some detective work.

"Just *how* did Kay's family get so rich?" I asked at dinner one night.

"From airline stock," said Seth. "They also own a Miami hotel and Lerner's Frozen Foods."

"You're never going to buy any of their stuff when we get a freezer, are you?" I said to Mom.

She shook her head. "Not if I can get Birdsall . . . I mean Birds*eye*."

Seth and I laughed, but Sarah was too busy thinking of something else. She fiddled with her fettucine, then she said, "Has anybody ever figured out *why* Kay wants to move to London?"

"Boredom, revenge . . . romance? Who knows?"

said Seth. "It's my guess that some of her jet-setter friends who live over there, talked her into it. She's always been attracted to their so-called glamorous social life."

Sarah shrugged. "But Kay goes to lots of parties here. R.J. told me she does. She's out almost every night."

He'd told me that, too. "My mother's a professional party-goer," was the way he put it, "that's why she usually sleeps till noon."

I don't think he minded not seeing her very much. Especially now, with the custody decision coming up. Every move of his made her suspicious. When she was home, she was on his back constantly, fighting with him.

Sarah and I only saw him once in the month between her birthday and the hearing in December. On weekends, she and I were in Croton. On Wednesdays, the weekday he was supposed to visit us, Kay purposely arranged to have him somewhere else.

One Wednesday she took him to get vaccinations and a passport photo.

To keep in touch, Sarah and I spoke to R.J. on the phone. We learned not to call in the afternoon. The first time Kay answered when I made a call, she said, "Who is this?" I told her Kitty and she said, "I'm sorry. R.J. isn't here." I knew he was, though.

The next time she answered, I disguised my voice. "This is Mrs. Snodgrass from National Family Opinion," I said, trying to imitate an old lady.

Kay hung up. It wouldn't have been so bad if she

had told me off, but she took the call out on R.J. and they had another fight. "From now on," she told him, "you can't receive any calls from either of those girls. And you can't call them."

We started calling each other just before bedtime when Kay was out for the evening.

R.J. was almost always down in the dumps when we spoke. The closer we got to the hearing, the worse he sounded. I talked to him about every cheerful subject I could think of—Shirley. Joy. Seth's new book contract. The tree at Rockefeller Center . . . Anything.

"Is your school having a special Christmas assembly?" I asked one night.

"We're doing the same old thing we always do," he said.

"What's that?"

"Singing about twenty carols in French and Latin and one token Hanukkah song in Hebrew. What about SCS? Are you doing anything special?"

I was hoping he'd ask. "My class is," I said. "We're putting on a play we wrote—'The Night Before Christmas in the Year 3001.' "

"Do you have a part?"

"Nope, something better," I said. "I'm in charge of sound effects. Got any suggestions on how I can do a spaceship?"

He had several. In the middle of describing what I could do for the takeoff and landing, I heard somebody at his house yelling:

"Is *this* how you carry on when I'm out? And just who are you talking to?"

"Kitty. We were only . . ."

A second later, we were cut off. Kay had come home early and caught him.

I have to admit she had me curious. I was dying to see her. She was such a rotten person, I pictured her as all dried up and warty-looking with mean eyes. But R.J. once told me she was pretty . . . "and very chic," he had added. I knew he hadn't said that to be bragging. Almost in the next breath, he told me he was certain she spent more money on clothes in a single month than their housekeeper lived on in a year.

After that, I pictured Kay as mean and warty-looking in spun gold ball gowns. What a surprise I was in for on December eleventh.

It was a Friday and the hearing started at two P.M. Seth and Mom picked Sarah and me up from school right after lunch. We drove straight to Centre Street and parked our car a block from the courthouse.

I could see the courthouse as soon as I got out of the car—a huge, no-nonsense gray building at the top of a mountain of steps. The bleak weather was a perfect backdrop.

None of us said much walking down the street. Sarah clomped her boots through the dirty, brown slush and Mom and Seth held hands, looking worried. I tagged behind feeling sorry for myself. I'd lost my gloves. I'd forgotten my boots. And my socks felt funny. Luckily I had on jeans and no one could tell that one sock was an ankle-high argyle and the other was a knee-high tube sock. Both were wet. I had holes in my sneakers.

My teeth chattered and I kept my head down against the wind until we crossed the street. When I looked up, I saw the words that were engraved in two-foot letters across the front of the courthouse:

WHEN JUSTICE ENDS . . . TYRANNY BEGINS

It was about as cheery as a warning label on a bottle of poison. But I was too cold not to go inside.

I followed a few feet behind Mom and Seth going up the steps. Sarah lagged a few feet behind me. "Hey, Kitty . . . Look!" she called. If I hadn't turned, I might have missed the long, black limousine that had pulled up to the curb.

A uniformed chauffeur got out and walked to the rear door. He bent slightly, like a coachman, opening it, and out stepped a tall, blonde woman wearing gray suede boots and a silvery fur coat that I recognized immediately as chinchilla. I'd once seen a live one in a pet shop.

The woman flicked some blonde hair off her shoulder, then turned. Was she gorgeous! . . . And I mean *movie-star* gorgeous. Until I saw her face, I never believed anyone could be more beautiful than the Breck Shampoo girls. Sarah and I couldn't stop staring. It was Kay.

I didn't make the connection until I saw R.J. climb out of the limousine after her. When he looked up, and our eyes met, I suddenly felt very awkward. I didn't know what to do. Should I wave? I wondered. Or should I pretend I didn't know him and dash up the steps after Mom and Seth? R.J. didn't seem to know what to do, either. He was biting his lip.

"Hey, R.J. . . . You'll never guess what happened this morning," Sarah called down to him. "Kitty dropped her socks in the toilet and they clogged it up and . . ."

It was true. I had. The darn things had accidentally flipped out of my hands when I stubbed my toe on the hamper. Then I'd accidentally flushed them. And they were my last pair of clean, matched socks.

But I could have kicked Sarah right down the courthouse steps for making it a public announcement.

I ran up the steps as fast as I could, not bothering to slow down when I passed Mom and Seth going in the doorway. I ran inside ahead of them and Mom hurried after me.

"Kitty, what's wrong?"

"Sarah!" I said. "She embarrasses me to death!"

Mom went pale. "Honey, please . . . Please don't fight with her today," she whispered. "Not today of all days."

I was calmer by the time we filed into Room 322 on the third floor. Something about being in a courthouse reminded me of a hospital. The smells are different—more of paper and leather and old wood and polish. But both places are quiet and people are serious.

Room 322 was the size of a small auditorium, with enough seats to accommodate a hundred spectators. We didn't expect more than a handful of people at the hearing. Only those of us who were personally involved in the case. Nobody else.

I sat between Mom and Sarah and looked around. The judge's bench, which is really a big desk, was up front on a platform. Behind it was an empty leather chair. The judge hadn't come yet. Sitting there, waiting for him, were a pitcher of ice water, a glass, a gavel and a name plaque that said, "Judge Greenwalt."

I looked at the empty chair, wondering if Judge Greenwalt was going to be a good judge. I hoped he was. And I hoped he wasn't biased about things like appearances. I've read that beautiful people are almost always given preferential treatment over plainer people.

Kay certainly knew she was beautiful. She walked into the courtroom with her head high and looked through Mom and Sarah and me like we were nothing more than three panes of glass. "You're going to sit over here," she said to R.J., directing him away from us.

Seth and his lawyer, who were talking to each other by the witness stand, got a frosty nod. But bing! A second later when she saw her own lawyer, Kay really turned on a dazzling smile.

It was one forty-five. "What do you think has happened to Mama and Papa?" I whispered to Mom.

"Relax, honey . . . They'll be here," she said. "They're probably parking their car."

"Too bad they don't have a limousine, huh?"

Mom smiled.

I hated myself for doing it, but I did it anyway. I stole another peek at Kay. My thousandth. She was taking off her chinchilla coat and I was hoping like crazy she'd be a big, fat tub of lard from the neck down. But, oh, no, her figure was terrific. A real eye-riveter, even covered with a plain gray cashmere sweater and skirt and a single strand of pearls.

It was a sin, I knew it was a sin, but now I was hoping the judge was blind.

Mama and Papa had come into the courtroom while I was busy watching Kay. I was so absorbed with her perfect long pink nails, I didn't see Mama and Papa sit down behind us, or talk to Mom and Sarah until Mama leaned forward. "How are you, darling?" she whispered to me.

"Fine," I said.

She sounded nervous. Papa looked solemn. No grandparents ever loved a kid more than they loved R.J. The judge's decisions were going to be very important to them. To all of us.

At one fifty-five, the secretary from R.J.'s school arrived. I knew she was coming. She had been subpoenaed to testify about Kay's request to have R.J.'s records sent to the Lathrop Boys Academy.

Kay gave her a cold look. Now she knew who had told Seth she was moving.

At two P.M. on the button, Judge Greenwalt entered the room in a billowy black robe. *She* was my second surprise for the day. She looked to be in her mid-fifties, had short, neat gray hair and wore her glasses on a chain below her white collar. From the brisk way she stepped up to her bench, she reminded me of my old principal in Briarcliff who never missed a trick.

She surveyed the eleven of us assembled and said, "Are we ready to proceed?"

The two lawyers said we were.

The first witness on the stand was the school secretary. Her testimony was brief and to the point. She said that Kay had requested her to send R.J.'s records to the Lathrop Boys Academy. It was her understanding that R.J. would be transferred there.

Kay was next. She walked to the witness stand looking confident and gorgeous, but Judge Greenwalt wasn't watching. She was pouring herself a glass of ice water.

Kay sat down, took an oath to tell the truth, then Seth's lawyer began questioning her.

Q: Have you ever been in London, Mrs. Krampner?

A: Yes.

Q: This year?

A: Yes.

Q: When?

A: In August.

Q: For how long?

A: Eight days.

R.J. perked up his head as he listened. I was sure he hadn't known about Kay's trip. She had gone to London while he was in camp and never told him.

Q: Wasn't your purpose in going there to find a residence for you and your son?

A: I was visiting friends.

Judge Greenwalt tapped her gavel. "Answer the question," she said to Kay.

Kay's blue eyes looked angry.

A: My answer is *no!* It was strictly a pleasure trip.

Seth's lawyer's next set of questions were tougher. He wanted to pin Kay down so she would have to admit she had applied to the Lathrop Boys Academy with the intention of transferring R.J. there. Kay made a flat denial. She said she had applied solely to satisfy her curiosity.

Q: Your *curiosity*, Mrs. Krampner? Would you explain that to the court?

A: Yes, of course. (Kay smiled.) I've always heard that American schools fall short of European standards. By applying to the academy, I learned that my son qualified for an equivalent grade level in the British school system. He's a very good student . . . He may want to continue his education abroad when he's older.

Judge Greenwalt slipped her glasses onto her nose and wrote notes without the slightest change of expression.

We were getting down to the nitty-gritty part. Seth's lawyer had done his detective work. He put his hand on the side of the witness stand and looked directly at Kay.

Q: You've scheduled another "pleasure trip" to London on December sixteenth, isn't that correct?

A: It is.

Q: And you're going there with your son?

A: I am.

Q: And you intend to return to the United States with him ten days later?

A: I do.

Q: So there would be no reason for you to withdraw any large sums of money from your New York bank account?

A: No, there would not be.

Now Seth's lawyer smiled.

Q: Really, Mrs. Krampner? Then would you please tell the court why you transferred *three hundred thousand dollars* to the London branch of First National on October fifteenth of this year?

Kay looked daggers at him, but she didn't squirm. She smoothed a fold in her skirt and sat up taller.

A: I've made that money available to David Atwood, a close friend. He's opening an art gallery in Piccadilly and needed a loan.

Maybe she's telling the truth, I thought. Piccadilly was such a silly name, she never would have made it up.

"Your honor, I have no more questions," Seth's lawyer said to Judge Greenwalt.

Kay's lawyer had a chance to ask Kay questions of his own, but he said he was declining. So the next witness on the stand was Seth.

I heard Mom's breathing speed up as he took his oath and sat down.

"He's going to do fine," I whispered.

Her hands were clasped so tight her knuckles glowed. They stayed that way throughout his entire testimony. In the first half he came off as a loving father who had a wonderful home to share with his son. That's when *his* lawyer was doing the questioning.

Then things got hairy. Kay's lawyer took over. He knew all about Soho and our building. And he was no Mr. Nice Guy! The way he phrased his questions, he made our loft sound like a pigsty located in the Black Hole of Calcutta.

Q: I understand your address is Sixteen Greene Street. Isn't that an old, defunct shoe factory, Mr. Krampner?

A: Yes. We're in the process of renovating.

Q: I see. How many rooms do you have completed at present?

A: Three.

Q: Is one a living room?

A: No.

Q: A dining room?

A: No.

Q: A kitchen?

A: No.

Q: *Oh?* What appliances do you use when you prepare meals at home?

A: At present, a toaster oven and a hot plate.

Q: I see. And *where* and upon *what* do you eat these toaster-oven meals?

A: Right now, on a drawing board set up in our hallway.

Q: Hmmm. May I ask if you *sit* while you eat, Mr. Krampner? And if so, upon what?

A: We have a mix of chairs and packing crates.

Q: Very interesting. How many children live with you and your wife?

A: My two stepdaughters.

Q: What pets do they have?

A: A dog and a cat.

Q: Isn't it true that your son has a pronounced fear of elevators?

A: Yes.

Q: And isn't it also true, Mr. Krampner, that the elevator currently in use in your building is a large, antiquated freight elevator with mesh sides and no top?

A: Yes.

Q: (Said very sarcastically) This is beginning to overwhelm me. Are you *really* asking the court to allow your son—who now lives in a luxury ten-room duplex *garden* apartment—to share three rooms in an old shoe factory with a dog, a cat and four other people . . . ride an antiquated freight elevator and eat toaster-oven meals sitting on a packing crate? *Isn't it a little too cramped at the Krampners to add another Krampner, Mr. Krampner?*

The smart aleck! He knew very well we wouldn't live that way forever. And Judge Greenwalt was laughing. I could have popped her on her nose.

We sounded like hobos. Kay's lawyer seemed satisfied and said he had no more questions for Seth. It was late. I thought the hearing was over, but Judge Greenwalt tapped her gavel, announcing that court was adjourned until ten A.M., Monday.

I asked Mom why. "Who else is going to testify?"

"Mama and Papa and I are," she said.

Leaving the courtroom, I looked for R.J. He was gone. Kay had high-tailed him out of there to avoid us. I didn't see them until the rest of us were going out the main door. They were almost at the bottom of the steps, heading for their limousine. Kay had her hand on R.J.'s shoulder, hurrying him.

"Kay . . . Wait!" Seth called after her. "I want a word with R.J. before you leave!"

Kay either didn't hear, or pretended she didn't. But R.J. had. He brushed her hand away—knocked it off, really—and came rushing up the steps, two at a time, to meet Seth halfway. I got a lump in my throat watching them. They talked a minute, then R.J. went back down the steps. He held his head like a flag at half-mast.

I knew it was going to be a down-in-the-dumps weekend.

...17

Sarah and I didn't go to court on Monday. Mom and Seth were afraid the hearing might drag on for days, so they sent us to school.

I couldn't do a bit of work. During math, my teacher, who knew where I'd been on Friday, saw me doodling stars and squiggles on the edge of my paper. "You look worried, Kitty . . . Is it about the custody hearing?"

I nodded. "My Mom's testifying today. I'm scared the other lawyer's going to make fun of her."

"If he tries, the judge will see right through him," she said. "Sarcasm is a bad substitute for a good defense."

That made me feel better.

As it turned out, my first impression of Judge Greenwalt was right. She was shrewd. After she had listened to all the testimonies, she asked to speak to

R.J. alone in her chamber. When they came out, an hour later, she had made her decisions.

She was announcing them in the courtroom at the exact same time Sarah and I were getting out of school. Of course neither of us had any way of knowing, so we didn't expect anyone to be calling us with good news when we unlocked the door to the loft.

"You girls are wanted on the phone," a carpenter was hollering.

I found him sitting on a stack of lumber, holding the phone. Papa was on the line.

"We won," Papa said. "We won *both* decisions!"

"You mean Kay can't take R.J. to London even for Christmas?" I asked.

"That's right."

Papa was calling from a courthouse pay phone and he was too excited to go into more detail. "We'll tell you everything when we see you," he said.

Sarah and I zoomed into action. R.J. needed a bedroom. Since we only had three—hers, mine and Mom and Seth's—somebody would have to double or triple up.

"And you know darn well Mom and Seth will want one of us to," said Sarah.

I told her I was too old to share with a boy, so she should share. She said I should. She was too young. Neither of us would give in and let the other one have a room to herself. We haggled and argued until the carpenters stopped working and stepped in to referee us.

"Look . . . Wanna know how each of you can keep the other from winning?" one of them said.

"How?" we asked.

"By letting that other kid—what's his name, R.J?—have a room to himself."

We hadn't thought of that. But we agreed it was the only solution. To decide whether we shared my room or Sarah's, we flipped a coin. She stayed and I moved, but she had to make two concessions—I got the top half of her dresser and the bed next to the window.

With that settled, we went to work. She cleared out my closet. I cleared out my drawers and gathered my stuffed animals. Together we carried in my doodad shelf that I use for my miniature animal collection.

We were just starting to empty my bookcase when we heard the front door open. We dropped books and ran to tell R.J. his room was almost ready. Then we saw that he hadn't come home with Mom and Seth. Only Mama and Papa had and they all seemed tired.

"Hey . . . Why didn't R.J. come?" said Sarah. "Did the judge change her mind?"

Seth shook his head. "No, honey . . . she didn't. My custody doesn't start for another thirty days."

"He'll be moving in by the middle of January for sure?" I asked.

"Unless Kay appeals," said Seth. "And I'm certain she will."

He didn't have to explain what "appeal" meant.

Sarah and I knew. When you're unhappy with a judge's decision, you take your case to a higher court called the Court of Appeals. There, five judges go through the case all over again.

Sarah and I groaned. An appeal could take months.

"The judge was dumb letting Kay keep R.J. over Christmas," said Sarah. "She might sneak him off to London even if she's not supposed to."

Seth helped Mom hang up Mama and Papa's coats. "She can't, Sarah . . . Judge Greenwalt made her turn over R.J.'s passport. Without one, he can't leave the country. So if Kay still wants to go to London, well . . . She'll have to go alone."

And she did. But not as early as she would have liked; she had to wait until her lawyer started the appeal proceedings. That delayed her departure by two days and she left the morning of December eighteenth.

R.J. came to stay with us.

His school was dismissed for the holidays at noon that day, the same as SCS. Seth drove uptown to hear his class sing French and Latin carols. And Mom came to SCS to see "The Night Before Christmas in the Year 3001."

I was sorry R.J. missed my sound effects. To get them, I borrowed Mordecai's tape recorder. Then I followed R.J.'s suggestion and rode up and down our freight elevator recording the screeching and grinding of metal. It was very effective. Played over the school microphone, it made all the little kids in the audience scream. For a few minutes they really thought Santa's spaceship was going to get sucked into a black hole in space.

Only two kids in the audience, besides Sarah, laughed. Max and Mordecai. They recognized our elevator.

By late afternoon, the play seemed a month behind me. R.J. had settled into my room, unpacked and fed Shirley. Mom and Seth had spent a few solid hours working. And Sarah and I had located our boxes of Christmas tree ornaments. We had all decided that this year we would combine Hanukkah and Christmas to suit us. Now it was time to start. Seth put his brass menorah on the windowsill, we lit the first Hanukkah candle and R.J. told us the story of the Maccabees.

Then we went out to buy our tree.

We got an enormous eight-footer for half price. It had big, full branches and needles as long as my fingers. The guy selling trees on Mercer Street said he'd marked it down because it was too tall for most apartments. He didn't mention the defect. It leaned. A lot.

We didn't notice until we had it home in a stand. Mom said we'd have to keep it and make believe it was normal. In a couple of days we were used to it.

Meantime, R.J., Sarah and I were making presents. Mom promised us that if we agreed to an old-fashioned Christmas, we could use her art supplies and take buttons, beads or anything we wanted from her carton of craft materials.

I knew why. We were getting short of money. She and Seth didn't talk about it, but the hearing had taken up a big chunk of what they'd saved for renovations. The appeal would take another big chunk. We needed to scrimp.

Mom took on an extra book jacket assignment and Seth worked day and night on his new book. To keep out of their hair, we three kids busied ourselves with our old-fashioned Christmas. Each of us staked out an unused corner of the loft and rigged up our own tent with packing crates and sheets. Then we worked secretly inside.

The only thing we showed each other were cards. R.J. made the best. My favorite was the one he was sending to Dr. Mendelmann. On the outside he drew a shrink with his eyes closed lying on a couch. On the inside he wrote, "God rest ye, Jerry Mendelmann."

I had a sneaky feeling that he and Sarah were working together on my present. They kept going inside each other's tents. Then one day, without telling me, they went across the hall and buzzed the Lebowitzes. Instead of coming back, they went outside.

I watched them cross the street from our front window. They had a big brown bag with them and I wanted to see where they were taking it. Aha! To Lottie's shop! So they're collecting something for me,

I thought. Then I decided they probably weren't. They were probably going to see Lila.

I'd already made most of my presents. They ranged from hand-painted barrettes to bead necklaces to a rag doll for Josh. Mama and Papa were getting the ceramic owl I'd glazed in art and Dad was getting my school picture. The homemade part was the frame; I'd glued seashells all over it so it would look nice in his office.

R.J.'s present was the most unusual—I was giving him a rock. I'd found it a long time ago in Briarcliff and kept it because it was as smooth and big as an ostrich egg. I knew someday I'd think of something to do with it. My flash came just before Christmas. After I gave it two coats of shellac, I borrowed Mom's red nail polish and painted "Roll me over" on the top and "Now tickle my tummy" on the bottom.

I was waiting to make Seth's present. He likes cookies and I planned to bake him a few at a time in our toaster oven the day before Christmas. Then something arrived to change my plan.

Three days before Christmas, Mom finished her new book jacket. The following day, we had two deliveries. The one in the morning was a full-sized refrigerator with a freezer and an ice-maker. It caused a sensation. For six months we had been using a dinky little office refrigerator from Seth's old apartment.

The new refrigerator was plugged into the space reserved for it in our future kitchen. When the ice was ready, I made a pitcher of iced tea and passed it around. Nobody wanted any. They all wanted canned sodas. I drank my iced tea by myself and thought mean things.

I was just getting over being mad when the second delivery came. It was a four-burner range with a self-cleaning oven. I thought Mom had ordered it as well as the refrigerator. Then I saw the card taped to the oven door. It was a Hanukkah gift to all of us from Mama and Papa.

As soon as the range was hooked up, I baked Seth a batch of chocolate macaroons on a regular baking sheet. When they cooled off, I wrapped them in colored cellophane and went inside my sheet tent to make a card. "To someone with a lot of Seth appeal," it said. "Yum, yum—XXX, Kitty."

We celebrated our old-fashioned Christmas on Christmas Eve. Mom and Seth cooked a stuffed goose in our new range. It looked greasy and disgusting and I wasn't going to touch it. Then I thought of the famine in Zaire and I ate goose. But I hated it.

After dinner, we sat around our tree and opened presents. Sarah thought the unicorns I'd painted on her barrettes were pigs, but she said she still liked them. And I knew R.J. loved his rock. Every time he tickled it, he laughed.

I was crazy about the purple scarf and mittens Mom knitted me. Purple's my best color. I gave her a kiss and she gave me one back for her bead necklace. Seth's present to me was funny. He had made a three-by-five foot poster of a picture of me scratching my knee at the wedding.

There was only one present left.

It was in a box big enough to hold a robe and it was for me. It had to be. R.J. and Sarah looked as if they were getting a fatal case of ants in the pants waiting for me to open it.

I let out a shriek as I ripped off the red wrapping paper. "So *this* is why you guys went to see Lottie last week," I screamed. Never, but never, never, *never* would I have guessed. The two of them had made me a genuine soda can flip-top vest!

Sarah was quick to tell me that Lottie had only helped a little bit. "She showed us how to put it together, but we did all the collecting," she said.

"And we offered to pay her," said R.J., "but she wouldn't accept anything."

"Especially when she heard why you didn't get a vest for your birthday," said Sarah.

I got so excited trying it on, I didn't notice it had a little something extra in the back till R.J. stood me still and pulled it over my head. A sleek, silvery, tight-fitting hood! Not a hair on my head showed.

While Seth took pictures of me modeling the vest with my hood up and my hood down, Sarah and R.J. told me how they thought the idea up together on my birthday. The next day they started collecting flip tops.

"It's amazing how many people contributed," said R.J. "The Lebowitz kids, Dr. Mendelmann . . ."

". . . and my teacher and the poet who got stuck with us in the elevator," said Sarah.

184

"And the guy taking these pictures," said Seth.

"And the woman standing next to him," said Mom.

"And we're never drinking another soda," they all said together.

Well, it's the vest to end all vests. I loved it so much I slept with it next to my pillow. I would have worn it, but it felt scratchy over my nightgown.

...18

The vest felt fine over a heavy wool ski sweater, Christmas morning. I put it on first thing, wore it for breakfast and I was still wearing it when we took the train to Croton. By "we," I mean Sarah, me *and* R.J. Dad and Linda had called during the week to invite him for Christmas dinner. He was spending the day with us.

"Did Linda mention we were having a little open house, this afternoon?" Dad asked when he picked us up at the station.

Sarah nodded. "She said a bunch of old friends were coming over."

"What about the Shapiros . . . Are they?" I asked.

"Except for Minna's brother," said Dad. "He's got the flu."

On the way to the house, Dad asked R.J. how his nose had been since the car accident. I'd almost forgotten. That hospital trip seemed ages ago.

"Oh, it healed nicely, thank you, Dr. Birdsall," said R.J.

Dad smiled. "If you'd like, R.J., you can call me Bob."

"Or Bobeldoo," said Sarah.

We all laughed.

Peter and Sylvia were standing by the door waiting for us when we arrived. They were dressed up in party clothes and full of questions for R.J.

"Are you another brother?" asked Sylvia.

"Sort of, I guess," said R.J.

"What would you like to see first?" said Peter. "The toys Santa brought us, or our baby brother?"

"I think R.J. would like to come in first and take off his coat," Linda said.

She and Dad couldn't have been nicer. They treated R.J. like one of us. Within minutes he relaxed and felt at home, which made me feel good. But I wasn't kidding myself. If they had treated R.J. like family a year earlier, when I first knew him, it would have made me mad.

I watched Dad hang coats in the closet, wondering if he had known then. Probably. That's why he and Linda had waited till now to invite R.J. to Croton.

Dad looked at my vest and held up a hanger. "What about you, Kitty? Can I take your . . . uh, shining armor?"

"No, thanks," I said. "I'm wearing it to show Minna."

I stationed myself on the couch by the front window waiting for the Shapiros' car to pull up. I hadn't seen Minna since the week after Josh came home from the hospital, three months before. I couldn't wait.

When I saw their car, I ran outside, nearly knocking Minna over, rushing to meet her. I recognized a lot of changes. Her orthodontist had taken off her train tracks—her teeth looked terrific. So did her hair. It had grown a couple of inches in the back and the sides were feathered.

"You look terrific . . . really *chic*," I said, borrowing one of R.J.'s words.

"Yeah, you too! Absolutely *fan*-tastic!" she squealed. She must have circled me twice, admiring my vest. "Wow! I can't believe it . . . actual flip tops! And what a great hood! *Hey, Mom . . . Turn around a minute,*" she called to Mrs. Shapiro who was taking little steps up the icy path with Mr. Shapiro. "Look what Kitty's wearing . . . Isn't it fantastic? *Now* do you see what I mean? The styles *are* better in New York than they are in Briarcliff!"

Mrs. Shapiro wasn't quite so enthused. She looked, but she didn't rave.

"She has totally no taste," Minna whispered.

When we got in the house, we found Sarah on the floor with Peter and Sylvia, playing with their new toys. She acted as if she were enjoying Sylvia's doll buggy more than Sylvia was.

"Where's R.J.?" I asked. "Minna wants to see him."

Peter was the only one who looked up. "He's in Josh's room."

R.J. didn't hear Minna and me open the door. He was sitting in the rocking chair, holding Josh in his arms. "John Jacob Jingle-Heimer Schmidt," he was singing away, "that's my name toooo . . . Whenever we go out, the peop . . ."

He clammed up the instant we giggled. We hadn't meant to, but his voice was so off-key, we couldn't help it.

"I didn't know you were listening," he said.

Josh was furious. I swear if he had been able to talk, he would have yelled at Minna and me for interrupting. He wouldn't stop crying.

R.J. looked helpless, rocking him. "Do you think he wants me to start singing again?"

Minna and I said we were sure he did and offered to join in to form a trio. We sang and we sang and we sang. After we ran out of Christmas carols, we sang nursery songs. After we ran out of those, we sang anything we could think of.

> *"Dirty Lil, dirty Lil*
> *lives on top of Garbage Hill.*
> *Never washes, never will . . .*
> *Oops, peeiouwy, dirty Lil."*

R.J. sat that one out since he didn't know it and Minna and I sang it twice. Little Josh seemed to hang on to every word.

"It's incredible . . . He's so young, yet he's already developed an ear for music," R.J. said.

Josh zonked out after "Yankee Doodle Dandy." We put him in his crib and went into the bedroom that Sarah and I shared. There were too many grownups in the living room to want to go out there.

"It must be great having a room here and another one in the city," said Minna.

R.J. looked at me and we both smiled. "Kitty gave up her other room," he said.

"You did, Kitty?" said Minna. "Why?"

I realized she didn't know anything about the hearing. I asked R.J. if he would mind if I told her.

"No, go ahead if you want," he said, as if he were surprised that I hadn't already.

The three of us sat on my bed while I brought Minna up to date. After I finished, she wasn't interested in why I gave up my room. She wanted to know what had gone on between Judge Greenwalt and R.J. in the judge's chamber.

"What did you tell her in there? That you wanted to live with your dad?"

"And a few other things," he said.

"Like what? That your mom was fibbing about her three hundred thousand dollars?"

"No, I think that part of her testimony was true. Well, *almost* true."

"I thought so," I said. "She doesn't look the type to make up a name like Piccadilly."

"Piccadilly?" said Minna.

R.J. laughed. "Yeah, there really is such a place. That's where my mother and David Atwood are opening their art gallery. They're going fifty-fifty on it. It's a partnership."

"But she told the judge he needed a loan," I said.

"David Atwood doesn't need loans, Kitty. His father's an earl. They're very wealthy."

"Do you know them?" asked Minna.

R.J. shook his head. "Only David. He's been to New York a few times to see my mother." He looked down at his lap a minute, then he glanced over at me. "I guess I forgot to tell you this, Kitty . . . They're getting married."

"*Married? Who? . . .* Your mother and David Atwood? She told you?"

R.J. looked as if he had a bad taste in his mouth. "No, André, her hairdresser told me. The day before she flew to England."

"But how did he know?"

"Oh, for pete's sakes, Kitty," said Minna, "women tell their hairdressers everything."

"Well, how did André happen to tell *you?*" I said to R.J. "Does he cut your hair?"

"No, he gives me facials."

He was kidding, of course, and we all laughed. Then he got serious again. "Actually, my mother sent me to his salon . . . She was too busy to pick up some earrings she'd left. When André gave them to me, he made a slip-up. He didn't know I didn't know about the wedding."

"Boy," said Minna, "the way you find out about things is the rock-bottom pits."

"Yeah, the rock-bottom pits," agreed R.J.

We stayed in the bedroom talking throughout the entire open house. After R.J. told Minna what might happen at the appeal, I asked her what had been happening on Hastings Street. Nobody's better at passing on news. She told me the Millens had been burglarized on Thanksgiving and that the people who moved into my old house had blacktopped their driveway.

"Oh, and this might interest you," she said, "he's going to Smoke-Enders and she's going to Weight Watchers."

A few minutes later, Mrs. Shapiro knocked on my door, telling Minna it was time to leave. I think R.J. was almost as sorry as I was. Both of us walked her to the car and stood, waving, at the curb as it pulled away.

It was the last car to leave. Minna rolled down her window and waved back. "Good luck on the appeal," she called to R.J.

I couldn't believe Sarah and Sylvia were still playing dolls. Peter, on the other hand, had grown tired of his Big Joe's Service Station. He wanted R.J. and me to play Chinese checkers with him. We did, but I could hardly concentrate. I hadn't eaten any of the hot hors d'oeuvres Linda had served at the party. And I was starving. All afternoon I'd smelled the good smells coming from the kitchen. We were having turkey for dinner. I was sure of it. My mouth watered, thinking how it would taste.

When Linda finally opened the sliding doors to the dining room, I was the first person in there. The table took my breath away it looked so snazzy. She had it set with white, lace-edged napkins on a crimson cloth that fell to the floor like a skirt. In the middle of a holly centerpiece, several tall, bayberry-scented candles were burning. And to the side of each plate was a little Christmas tree made out of green gumdrops.

Sylvia reached for R.J.'s hand. "Mommy says I can sit next to you."

"And me, too," said Peter.

R.J. sat between them, enjoying the fuss they were making. He liked being the new "other" brother. I sat across from the three of them, next to Sarah. My stomach growled as I watched Dad come from the kitchen carrying a big platter.

"Kitty, your rumblings abdominal are simply phenomenal," he teased.

"I know . . . I could eat a horse," I announced.

When I saw what was on the platter, I could have bitten off my tongue. We were having goose! Another gross, disgusting roast goose.

Linda smiled as Dad began carving. "I thought we'd try something different this year."

That's exactly what Mom had said the night before. Each of them had thought the other was fixing us turkey. Rats! I ate. Not because I wanted to, but because Linda had gone out of her way to make this a perfect day.

"Mmmm, the goose is delicious," I said, trying not to get sick, swallowing.

That got me a funny look from Sarah and R.J. They thought I'd gone crazy.

Plum pudding for dessert killed the taste. After

we finished it, Sylvia led us into the living room to open presents. "See," she said to R.J. "Santa knew you were coming."

I hadn't noticed earlier, with so many people around, but there were six red felt stockings hanging from the fireplace mantel. R.J.'s was next to Josh's, with his name on it, and it was filled with presents, just as Sarah's and mine were.

He couldn't get over the stopwatch he found way down in the toe. He rubbed it between his fingers, wound it and let Peter and Sylvia listen to it tick. "I've always wanted one," he told them. "I wonder how Santa Claus knew . . . I've never told anybody."

He hasn't gone anywhere without it since.

Dad drove Sarah, R.J. and me back to New York City, that night, but before we left, Linda bundled Josh in his little blue snowsuit and all eight of us went for a long Christmas ride. Peter sat on R.J.'s lap, Sylvia on mine, both pressing their noses against the cold car windows.

The decorations on the houses we passed weren't much different from the ones I remembered in Briarcliff. We saw smiling Santas and reindeer, candy canes and choir boys, a manger on a bank of snow and lots of trees strung with lights. What I liked was the sameness.

From the top of Croton's highest hill, we could look down on the black waters of the Hudson River. A single steam trawler was making its way toward the New York harbor. Along the banks on the other side, lemon-colored lights were flickering.

"Those people over there are saying 'Merry Christmas' to us," I told Sylvia.

She giggled. "Kitty, you goofus . . . They turn their lights on *every* night!"

She was five and not so easy to fool. The pompom on her hat bobbed against my chin as she sat back. "When're you coming again?"

"Soon," I said.

She patted my hand with her mitten. "Good. I like it when you're here."

So did I. It was fun being with all my brothers and sisters.

...19

"Is Kay really married?" Sarah would ask.

Then both of us would chime: "Only her hairdresser knows for sure."

That was our private joke after Kay came back from England. If she had married David Atwood, she wasn't telling. From all appearances, her two-week trip to London was just for "pleasure." Then she returned to the States promptly at the end of December, as she had testified at the hearing.

R.J. had to move back in with her until his custody was settled at the appeal in March. I moved out of Sarah's room and back into my own. Mom and Seth assured me I could stay there for good. Enough money had come in from Seth's latest magazine articles so that we were able to go ahead and do more work on the loft. We were installing a complete kitchen and walls were going up for two more rooms. One room was to be R.J.'s.

Sarah and I were sure the small corner room next to his would be a place where we could watch TV. But sometime late in February we learned that Mom and Seth had another purpose in mind. They were turning it into a nursery; Mom was pregnant.

As thrilled as Sarah and I were about the baby, our excitement was no match for R.J.'s. He went bonkers. The way he catered to Mom when he came over, he acted like a little old nanny.

"May I get you another cup of tea, Liz?"

"No . . . Don't move that chair, Liz! I'll move it."

"Liz, don't you think you should get off your feet now?"

"You're cooking? Are you *sure* your doctor knows you're cooking?"

The nanny stuff got to me. After a couple of visits from him, I was fed up with it. "Look, R.J.," I told him one night when he insisted on frying chicken for her, "Mom's *not* an invalid!"

"I know she isn't," he said, "but she *is* thirty-seven, Kitty. And she *is* in a delicate condition. And it's really time you started being more considerate of her."

"Oh, yeah? How?" I asked.

I should have known better. He told me. With a hundred and one helpful household hints, he told me. Then he added that I ought to take the garbage out to the stairwell when he wasn't around to do it.

"She shouldn't be lifting," he said.

That led to our first clash in months.

"Sure! It's easy for you to criticize," I shouted. "You don't have to do anything when you're home except your homework. You've got a *housekeeper!*"

I made "housekeeper" sound as bad as a hired gangster. R.J. looked hurt, but I didn't care. He'd hurt me worse suggesting I wasn't concerned about Mom.

I refused to eat his fried chicken and stormed off to my room to sulk. I sat on my bed in the dark over an hour, thinking. For the first time since the hearing, I wasn't sure if I wanted Seth to win custody of him.

"*Kitty?* May I come in and talk to you a minute?"

R.J. was outside my door. It was time for Seth to take him home, but I was in no mood to say goodbye. I kept quiet.

"Kitty . . . *Please?* I won't see you till the appeal and I want to tell you something."

"What? How lazy I am?"

"No, not at all," he said. "And I'm sorry I was critical . . . Liz talked to me about it at dinner. She says I overdo being helpful."

"She *did?*" I couldn't believe Mom was on my side. "What else did she say?"

"That it'd be nice if you and I hit a happy medium. That maybe you could be a little more helpful and I . . ."

"Is *that* what you wanted to tell me?" I snapped.

"No."

"Well, if you have to come in, come in!"

As he opened my door I quickly grabbed a book and turned on my table lamp. I didn't want him to know I'd been sulking in the dark.

He smiled. "Do you always read upside down?"

I flipped my book rightside up and looked at him. "*Well-l?* What is it?"

He sat on the bed next to me, holding his overcoat. "I don't want to leave here with any bad feelings between us," he said. "The appeal's next week, you know."

I nodded.

"It's the end of the line . . . It makes everything final. My mother's very confident. She expects to win. And if she does," he went on, "I won't be seeing you very much. Probably once or twice a year during vacations, is all . . . Lathrop Academy is a boarding school."

I shrugged. "You won't be going there unless your mother moves," I said. "And she may decide not to."

"Oh, she'll move. Win or lose, with or without me, she'll be in London to marry David Atwood as soon as the appeal's over."

I looked at him out of the corner of my eye. "What makes you so sure she didn't get married at Christmas?"

"Because she's too smart. The wedding would've made the papers . . . the society columns," he said. "And that wouldn't have looked good after what she testified at the hearing. She's waiting."

"Who told you? Her hairdresser?"

R.J. laughed. "He didn't have to . . . She's my mother. I know how she thinks. And I know she does whatever she wants."

"Well, she sure must want you," I said. "Why else would she be going through all this trouble?"

"*Why?*" He rubbed his thumbnail. "Because she's a person who just can't stand losing. The appeal's only a game to her, Kitty . . . She wants to win for the sake of winning. To beat Dad."

He was quiet and I was quiet. I'd forgotten I was mad at him and closed my book. We were quiet some more until he glanced over at me.

He was smiling. "Anyway, telling you all that isn't the reason I came in here," he said. "What I really wanted to tell you was . . . well, two things, actually. Remember the first time you and Sarah had dinner at Mama and Papa's?"

I told him I did.

"And I wouldn't let Mama tell you the story of how I got the name R.J.?"

"Yeah, you shrieked your head off," I said.

"Well, now I'm going to come clean. The J stands for Jacob. That's the name on my birth certificate."

I was disappointed. "I've heard of names a lot more nauseating."

"So have I. But you haven't heard the *other* half of the story . . ."

"You mean the R part?"

He nodded. "You see, when I was little, Mama and Papa were always talking about a Jewish rabbi they liked . . . a Rabbi Jacobs. I thought his name meant me. And I got so used to hearing 'Rabbi Jacobs this' and 'Rabbi Jacobs that,' that when I went to nursery school, if the teacher said, 'That's Jacob's cubby over there,' I'd correct her and say, 'No! That's *Rabbi* Jacob's cubby!' "

"What did the kids in your class do? Start calling you Rabbi Jacob?"

"Sure. Then everyone else did. And sometimes I was known as 'Rabbit Jacob' or 'Rapid Jacob' . . ." He watched me flop back on the bed, laughing. "Or even *'Rabies* Jacob.' By the time I was in kindergarten, I hated my name. So I went by my initials."

"You numbskull! *R* isn't your initial!"

"I know," he said, laughing as hard as I was, "but until I was nine, that never occurred to me."

Both of us broke up all over again. He was hugging his sides and I was wheezing. I wanted to catch my breath so I could tell him about the battle I'd had in fourth grade with a kid in Briarcliff who used to call me "Kitty Litter."

I didn't have a chance. Someone out in the hall was knocking on my door. We sat upright and looked at it.

"R.J.," Seth called. "Come on . . . Say good night to Kitty. I've got to drive you home now."

I groaned. "So *soon?*"

"Right, honey . . . It's late. You both have school tomorrow."

"Just give me another minute," R.J. called.

The laughter in his voice was gone. I watched him put on his overcoat, waiting to hear the second thing he wanted to tell me. It wasn't going to be funny.

He fastened the top button on his coat, then hesitated. "You know, Kitty," he said as he fingered the next button, "I was a little put off by your personality when I first knew you. I didn't like you very much. I thought you were, uh, well . . . a terrible show-off."

That stung. He had no idea how much. I looked down at my hands. "I guess maybe I am sometimes."

"Oh, but you're not . . . not at all!" The bed bounced as he sat beside me again. "I just didn't understand you then," he said. "You're *naturally* vibrant. I think you're wonderful."

I looked up. "You *do?*"

"Yes, I do. I wish everybody could be like you— you never hide your feelings. And what I came in here to tell you was—if I could choose any sister in the world, I'd choose you."

...20

Kay lost the appeal.

It took the five judges two weeks to render their decision, and when they did, it was unanimous—Seth was to assume custody of R.J.

We heard the news from Seth's lawyer on St. Patrick's Day. I remember specifically because Sarah was watching the parade on TV and I was frosting shamrock sugar cookies when the call came. Seth was standing by, ready to answer the phone, as he had been every day since the appeal. First his lawyer congratulated him on winning, then he told him Kay had one week to turn R.J. over to us.

Instead, there was a terrible hullaballoo that night.

Just after midnight, the intercom buzzed from the lobby, waking me from a sound sleep. Joy went into a frenzy barking, then the phone in the kitchen and both extensions started ringing. Lights were flicked on in our hallway and there was a bong, bong, bong, bong coming from the doorbell.

The pandemonium meant one thing to me—that there was a fire somewhere in our building. I came rushing out of my room at the same time Sarah rushed out of hers carrying Flossie, the pink rabbit she'll probably be sleeping with when she's a senior citizen.

"Do you think we've got robbers?" she screamed.

I was too scared to think. Something that sounded like a bellyload of cargo from a Boeing 747 was being dumped in our foyer. The floor creaked under the weight of a heavy object getting shoved and pushed onto it. Whoever was doing it was grunting. Then a deep, nasal voice I didn't recognize said, "There's some more down in my trunk."

"Dead bodies," I whispered to Sarah. She screamed again.

Neither of us dared go out there to look. My heart was pounding so loud I wasn't sure if I heard other voices. But I thought I did.

Why weren't Mom and Seth answering the phone?

It had been ringing at least five minutes. Where were they? Their bedroom door was open. I was contemplating dashing in there to get the extension by their bed when Mom zipped down the hall past Sarah and me. She was in her fuzzy red robe and she was coming from the foyer.

"Who's been murdered?" Sarah yelled after her.

"Nobody. R.J.'s here," Mom called as she went in her room. "He just came in a taxi." Then she picked up the phone.

Sarah and I ran to the front door. We might have thought Mom was kidding if we hadn't stumbled across everything R.J. owned. Several suitcases and a typewriter were next to the closet. A stereo and a painting wrapped in a yellow bath towel were on a chair. In the middle of the floor was Shirley's cage surrounded by an assortment of shopping bags from posh stores like Henri Bendel's. Holding the front door open was a tan, leather trunk.

R.J. had disappeared.

"Where do you suppose he went?" asked Sarah.

"Downstairs with the driver to get the rest of his things."

"Then where's Seth?"

"Probably with them."

She started snooping in the shopping bags and I went out in the hall to see if the elevator was coming. It was the new, modern one that had been installed in February and it was so quiet, it was hard to tell if it was running or not.

I decided it wasn't and headed back for the loft. As I was about to come in, I noticed that the Lebowitzes' door across the hall was partially open. A bare foot was sticking out. It belonged to Bobo, Mordecai's three-year-old brother, who was in his blue flannel pajamas, eating a carrot.

"What're you doing up this late?" I asked.

"Watching," he said.

"Be a good boy . . . Go back to bed now," I told him.

He crunched down on his carrot, deciding. " 'Night," he said and shut the door.

When I went inside, Sarah was leaning out a living room window, yelling down to the street in a voice loud enough to be heard in Brooklyn. *"Hey . . . You guys need any help?"*

As I leaned out the window, I saw lights go on in the apartment over the health food store.

"We'll get dressed," she hollered.

Another light went on a couple of floors up from the African art gallery. Then another one above Lottie's shop.

"We've got everything," Seth answered. He sounded like he was at the bottom of a well.

A gust of wind whipped my hair on end. A second one made the sleeves of my nightgown dance. I shivered. Down on the street, parked next to the curb with its doors open, the jumbo yellow Checker cab looked the size of a bumblebee with spread wings. I felt dizzy and pulled my head back inside. At that moment I knew what R.J. meant by acrophobia.

Sarah and I were waiting by the elevator in our robes when he came up with Seth and the cabbie. He was so upset, I don't think he realized he'd just ridden in it. Helping him carry a box of books down the hall, I found out he'd had a terrible fight with Kay.

"What over? . . . The appeal?" I asked.

"That started it," he said.

More of the story unfolded when Mom got off the phone. All this time she had been talking to Kay who told her that R.J. had packed his things and moved out of their apartment while she was at the theater.

206

"Your mother said you didn't even leave her a note," she told R.J. Then she looked at Seth. "And she's insisting that you take him back . . . *Now*, Seth. She won't give him up until her custody ends next week."

"I don't care . . . I'm not going," said R.J.

He cried, confirming Kay's story. It was true. But what Kay hadn't told Mom, he said, was what had happened before she left for the theater. She had gone into a rage after her lawyer called to tell her she lost the appeal. Then she had turned on R.J.

"She accused me of betraying her at the hearing. Then she slapped me and said . . ."

The phone was ringing. Seth answered, certain it was Kay, and it was. I couldn't hear his half of the conversation because he was talking to her in the kitchen. When he came out, he said she had threatened to call her lawyer if he didn't bring R.J. home.

"What did you say?" asked Sarah.

"To go ahead and call."

Five minutes later Kay called again. Seth spoke to her, hung up, and she called right back. This time he let the phone ring and it kept ringing and ringing for twenty minutes. Finally he took it off the hook.

"Come on. It's late . . . Let's go to bed," he said.

R.J.'s new room was almost finished, except for being painted. Mom and Seth made up his bed while he and Sarah and I brought in Shirley and unpacked a couple of his suitcases. Then Sarah and I said good night. R.J. was still too keyed up to go to sleep, so Mom and Seth stayed in there to talk to him. Obviously, he wouldn't be going to school in the morning.

I don't know how long I'd been back to sleep when the second commotion broke out. The intercom buzzed from the lobby, then Joy went into another frenzy barking. I knew there wasn't a fire and I stayed in bed.

Coming home from school the next afternoon, Sarah and I found out we'd had a visit from Kay during the night. Mom hadn't mentioned a word about it at breakfast. But then, she'd been so groggy she'd poured orange juice on my cereal.

We heard about Kay's visit from Lottie.

She motioned for Sarah and me to come in her shop when she saw us stop to look at the harem pants she was displaying in her window for spring. They were made out of Army camouflage silk, she said. Then she told us our stepfather was some hip diplomat. "If you ask me, he should be appointed secretary general of the UN," she said.

Sarah and I must have looked puzzled.

"You mean he didn't tell you about last night? How he stopped a riot?"

We shook our heads.

"Whew! You're kidding?"

We said we weren't.

"Oh, yeah? He came down and cooled off the neighborhood hotheads at three A.M. Talked them out of damaging this la-di-da lady's big, black limousine . . ."

I had a queer sensation in my stomach. "What lady?"

Lottie laughed. "I don't know. Some spoiled duchess swathed in mink . . . real arrogant. She was parked in the middle of the street laying on her horn like she thought she could raise the sun with it. Wouldn't stop, either."

"Why didn't anybody call the police?" asked Sarah.

"Jimmy over the health food store hollered down and told her he was," said Lottie. "And it's what she yelled back that started the riot."

"What?" I asked.

"That if he did, she'd buy up the neighborhood buildings like trinkets and have everybody evicted. You better believe bottles were hurled out of windows over that. One hit her windshield, but she still kept honking. Your stepfather was the only one who could talk to her."

I knew why. And Sarah looked as if she were catching on. I hurried her out of Lottie's shop so fast she looked like the little road runner who goes beep-beep.

"Why do think Kay came down here?" she said as we crossed Greene Street.

Seth gave us the answer when we went upstairs: Kay was having a tantrum. First she'd lost the appeal, then R.J. had moved out. Discovering that Seth had taken our phone off the hook was the final straw.

"At that point she must have started drinking," he said. "She was two sheets to the wind when I talked to her over the intercom. And furious. She wanted me to bring R.J. down to the lobby in five minutes . . . and not a second longer. When I refused, she threatened to sit in her car and blow the horn. I didn't think she would, but she did."

"What did you say to stop her?" I asked.

"That I'd put in a long-distance call. To someone in Palm Springs."

"Who?"

"The only person she's afraid of. Her father."

This happened a little over two months ago. A few days later, Kay flew to London. Nobody was more surprised than R.J. when she called him in the middle of April, saying she was home. For good, she added. The next night she took him out to dinner to tell him that she had dissolved her partnership in the art gallery.

R.J. translated that as meaning she had decided not to marry David Atwood.

In my opinion, Kay came back to New York because she cares for R.J. a lot more than he's ever realized. Maybe even more than she's ever realized. Losing him may have knocked some sense in her head.

She's seeing a shrink on Fifth Avenue four times a week now. She started about the same time R.J. stopped his sessions with Dr. Mendelmann, which is a pretty interesting coincidence, I think. What's most important, though, is that R.J.'s relationship with her is improving.

Not long ago, Kay took him to an ice hockey game at Madison Square Garden, even though she's never been a hockey fan. R.J. never has been, either. Kay didn't know he disliked hockey when she bought the tickets. But at least she was trying.

We're not really cramped at the Krampners. Once the bedroom floors are scraped and we get rugs, the loft will be completely finished. Thirty two hundred square feet is plenty of space and we're all looking forward to the baby. We're going to name her Rachel.

I know that sounds funny. But the reason we know in advance she's a girl is that Mom had an amniocentesis, a test given to expectant mothers over the age of thirty-five. By analyzing a tube of fluid withdrawn from the sac where the unborn baby grows, doctors can determine a number of things about the baby. One is the sex.

I'm predicting that R.J. will drive me crazy doing his nanny routine with Rachel. He's already told Mom and Seth they'll never have to hire a baby sitter.

Living with him full time has called for a zillion major adjustments on my part. One is trying not to go to pieces waiting for him to finish waterpicking his teeth in the morning, so I can use the bathroom.

Another is overlooking his obsession with neatness.

Take the way he keeps his room. Last week, in a pinch, I borrowed his penny loafers because Joy had chewed up my sneakers and I couldn't find my clogs. I was careful to put the loafers back in his closet when

I took them off. But that wasn't good enough for R.J. Oh, no.

"Kitty, next time I'd appreciate it if you'd put them where they belong," he told me.

What he meant was, in alphabetical order in his shoe rack—between the L. L. Bean hiking boots he's never worn and his oxfords.

I know I've got a few petty, little faults of my own. (So I've been told.) And Sarah has more irritating faults and bad habits than there are stars in the heavens. Therefore I won't go into all of R.J.'s faults. Except to say if I had my "druthers," I'd druther he wouldn't time everything, and I mean *everything* (the toaster, traffic lights, TV commercials, etc. etc. etc.) with his stopwatch.

The elevator gets to me the most. If he isn't explaining how an overspeed activates the safety device, he's checking to see how fast we're traveling to the pit . . . *"Now we're eighty-three feet,"* he'll say, looking at his stopwatch. *"Now we're seventy-four feet. Now we're sixty-five feet . . ."*

When I'm in one of my more tolerant moods, I find having a live-in brother isn't so bad. It's fun, actually. R.J.'s an excellent listener. He's also got some amazingly good ideas. Like the swivel-peeling contest he organized when the four oldest Lebowitz boys were over yesterday.

He lined them and Sarah and me up along the kitchen counter, gave us each a plate, fork, serrated knife and an orange. Then with his own orange, he demonstrated how to cut off one long, continuous peel.

212

It isn't easy. Oranges wobble and it's against the rules to hold yours with your fingers. You have to stick your fork into the top, then turn the fork so the orange revolves slowly on your plate. As it turns, you cut off your peel with your knife, working your way from the top down to the bottom. The narrower the strip of peel is, of course, the longer it is. We were all trying for the longest.

I made mine no wider than a piece of spaghetti and it kept breaking off. Of the Lebowitz kids, Mordecai was the only one whose peel didn't break. His was ten inches long, but Sarah's won the contest. I never knew she had such powers of concentration. With those delicate little fingers Mama is always raving about, she worked painstakingly on her orange, cutting off a half-inch-wide strip from beginning to end. Laid out flat it measured nearly twenty-four inches.

None of us knew what to do with the seven left-over oranges, so R.J. suggested we add more fruit and make ambrosia. We ate it for lunch.

He and Mordecai hit it off right away. Mordecai wants to be an artist when he grows up. He likes R.J. to criticize his drawings because he thinks R.J.'s an art expert. Whenever they can, they go uptown to the Guggenheim Museum or the Museum of Modern Art. Sometimes I go with them. Sometimes I don't.

They're both wild about the work of a guy named Magritte whose idea of a painting was a room with nothing in it but a floor-to-ceiling apple. It's hard to tell if it's supposed to be a gigantic apple or a teeny little room. Either way you see it, you get an attack of claustrophobia.

My taste in art hasn't changed. I still prefer Norman Rockwell and the Breck Shampoo girls.

Last night I couldn't sleep. I sat at my window a long time, enjoying my view of Soho. It's more interesting than pretty. I like the gargoyles now. Sometimes I look at their faces through Seth's binoculars. And I'm always spotting something new, like the windmill I can see if I look to the right of the fire escape on Lottie's building. It's on a rooftop a block away and it's there for a purpose, R.J. says. It powers the building's generator.

When I got into bed, I realized how long it had been since I thought of my room in Briarcliff. From my window there, I could see our yard and our big, old weeping willow tree. I loved that tree. But I don't miss it much any more. Or even our house on Hastings Street. They seem far away. A lot of things do.

The saddest day of all my life, the day my dad moved out and I ran, crying, to the duck pond with Joy, seems as if it happened a lifetime ago.

Last night I thought of that day. I'd been so sure my heart would break when Mom and Dad broke the bad news—they didn't love each other, they said. And he was leaving. It was a lifetime ago, but I remember the sound of Mom's voice as she held Sarah and cried. I followed Dad upstairs and watched him pack. I asked if he would be moving away forever. He said he didn't know. But I knew.

214

I've never run faster than I ran to the duck pond. I ran faster than Joy. We sat in the damp marshes for hours, not bothering to go home for dinner. And I had been so sure, so absolutely certain I'd never be happy again.

Last night as I lay in bed remembering how sad I'd felt, I wished I could go back in time, knowing everything I know now. If I could, I thought, I'd go back to that day at the duck pond.

And I'd have a talk with myself.

"Now look, Kitty," I'd say, "you think because your dad is leaving, you're losing him. Well, you're wrong . . . He'll never stop loving you! Your life's just going to be different is all.

"Big changes are coming. And wonderful people are waiting to meet you. There's a photographer in your mom's future. A nurse in your dad's. There will be weddings and babies, new brothers and sisters, more grandparents to love you, crazy adventures and good times ahead. You'll be a bridesmaid. You'll move. And you'll go to court rooting for a pointy-nosed boy you met at a ballgame.

"And someday, not so many years from now, when you look back and ask, Would I change today if I could? You'll say, No . . . no, I wouldn't. It would mean never knowing all those new people I love.

"So don't cry, Kitty. You'll live through today. And tomorrow. And the next. But you won't stay sad. Just wait! Around the corner is a happy beginning."

Wally
Where the Elf King Sings
... *Also by Judie Wolkoff*